IRO:
Bo
BLIND PANIC
By A. J. Harlem

A. J. Harlem

Books by A. J. Harlem
Sin, Repent, Repeat
The Last Post
Blind Panic

BLIND PANIC: Text copyright © AJ Harlem 2020
All Rights Reserved

With the exception of quotes used in reviews, this book may not be reproduced or used in whole or in part by any means existing without written permission from AJ Harlem.

Warning: The unauthorized reproduction or distribution of this copyrighted work is illegal. No part of this book may be scanned, uploaded or distributed via the Internet or any other means, electronic or print, without the author's written permission.

This book is a work of fiction and any resemblance to persons, living or dead is purely coincidental. The characters are productions of the author's imagination and used fictitiously.

Chapter One

Manfred Napier removed his irritating safety goggles and glanced at the large black clock on the wall. Only two hours to go. Then he'd get himself home, put a meal for one in the microwave—it was Tuesday so that meant lasagne—and settle down to watch The One Show.

February the fifteenth would then be another day he could cross off the calendar. Retirement was only three months away. He could hardly wait. Three decades at Colour Me Happy was long enough for any mortal.

He carried on working the assembly line. As head of quality control he checked the aerosols, half and one litre paint pots, and the small testers slipping by. The labels had to be on straight, and the lids and valves needed to be up to standard. Most importantly he had to be sure there was no damage to the cans. That was vital—paint was a volatile mix of chemicals with a low flashpoint, and especially in the aerosols it required careful handling.

It was Desert Sunset's turn today, more commonly known as orange, and he checked each aerosol as it came down the line from Darrell, Terry, Fredrick, and Beryl, before placing it in Colour Me Happy boxes.

Happy, now there was a word. He'd be happy when he didn't have to get up with the birds each morning. He could sleep in, watch daytime TV, and then head down The Hanged Carpenter and play darts in the evening. He was good at darts, and on the pub team, the blokes were a laugh, too. Not like this lot here. Right miserable bunch. Terry was the worst, always moaning on about his arthritis. And when he started up, Beryl went in competition with him about her runny bowels. Darrell, his chief complaint was his lack of time to play golf and the price of running a car, and as for Fredrick, well, he'd get an Olympic medal in moaning. The ugly old twat whined about anything and everything. If the sun was out it was too hot, at Christmas he was the ultimate bah humbug, and if he took a holiday it gave him a month's worth of whingeing material when he returned. Right royal pain in the arse, that was what he was. If ever there was someone who deserved to drop down dead of a sudden, unexpected heart attack, it was him.

Manfred carried on working the assembly line, his mind wandering to the pretty barmaid at The Hanged Carpenter. She was married, but he'd heard a rumour it was on the rocks. She'd get snapped up quick. With bubbles of blonde hair, red lips made for kissing, and an arse just asking for a pinch, he'd have to get in quick and hope she liked an older man.

He chuckled to himself, remembering how she'd giggled the week before when he'd cracked a few jokes about the poncey royal family who were in the news yet again. Bloody freeloaders. Maybe he'd work on some more material for the next time he saw her, make her see he was a fun bloke. Just because he had a few grey hairs didn't mean he was past it. And so what that he'd had to start taking digoxin a few years ago for atrial fibrillation—bloody nuisance—his todger still rose to the occasion.

Now all he needed was the occasion.

"What are you laughing about, Mannie?" Terry called over from where he operated the filling machine.

Manfred gritted his teeth, and his smile fell. He hated being called Mannie, always had, but no amount of telling this dumb lot made any bloody difference. "Nothing," he muttered.

"Ah go on, tell us, we need a smile."

Huh, isn't that a true statement. Miserable bastards.

Manfred shrugged and ducked his head, carried on checking the Desert Sunset aerosols. The one he was holding appeared dented, bent at the top, too, near the valve. He examined it closer, peered at the seal.

A sudden, piercing boom accompanied the worst pain he'd ever known. White, searing-hot fire scorched over his face, drying his eyeballs, frying his skin. He heard his hair frazzle, and his scream was caught in the violent whoosh of burning air that forced its way down into his lungs.

It was as if he'd been whacked in the back by a herd of elephants as he hit the floor, the air now blasting up his windpipe. He shrieked and reached for his face. His skin was blistering hot, sticky, too. The agony was unreal, sizzling, as if he'd been dipped into a volcano and the lava was gluing to him.

He writhed, attempting to escape the agony, but it followed him. So did the torturous ring in his ears.

"Mannie, it's okay!" Someone was at his side, their voice distant, they could have been speaking through a solid oak door.

"Shit, his overall is on fire." Darrell's voice.

Rapid tapping on his right arm, then the hiss of an extinguisher.

"Help me!" he managed, his voice a gurgle of desperation. "Help me!"

"Someone call an ambulance," Terry shouted. "Now."

"I'm on it." Beryl.

"Argh!" Manfred wailed and screamed, twisting this way and that. The black torture had consumed him. It was all that existed. It was as if every other thought, memory, experience he'd ever had had been eradicated. This heart-stopping, awful moment was his universe.

Maybe my heart will give up.

Yes. Let me die. Let this end.

"You'll be okay, Mannie. Ambulance is on the way."

Be okay? Be fucking okay?

He shook, a full-body, bone-rattling tremble. Part pain, part fury—Darrell thought it would all be okay? His skin was on fire, his eyes unseeing, and his chest felt as though it was about to explode.

He continued to wail, only just hearing it over the screech in his ears.

"He's got something sticking out of his eye," Fredrick said.

"Leave it," Beryl said. "The doctors will take it out."

"Get rid of it," Manfred shouted, he hovered his shaking hands over his face. He couldn't see them, but he knew where they were. Maybe if whatever was in his eye was removed he'd see again. "Get fucking rid of it."

"No, we're not supposed to," Beryl said. "We might do more damage."

"It's a bit of the bloody aerosol can," Fredrick said, sounding fascinated. "The metal's stuck right in, look, it's glinting."

Manfred wailed again. His pulse was racing, his limbs tightening and contracting. It was hard to catch his breath.

"Here's the first-aid kit." Terry was at his right-hand side.

The first-aid kit didn't instil any hope in Manfred. What good would cotton wool, saline, and a goddamn sling and safety pins do?

"Should we throw some cold water on his face?" Fredrick asked.

"Bloody hell, didn't you go to that health and safety course?" Terry replied.

"I was only asking."

"We need to keep him warm, he's shaking," Beryl said. "Fredrick, you go and watch for the ambulance, bring the paramedics straight here."

"Yeah, I can do that."

"Terry, find a blanket, or coats, anything."

"Yep, okay."

Within seconds, heavy material was placed over Manfred, he didn't know what, but it did nothing to stop the vicious shaking that had taken control of all of his nerve endings. His teeth clattered, and his ribs, jaw, and spine hurt.

"Try and relax," Terry said. "Help is on the way."

It seemed as if the fury those stupid words sent searing through Manfred was every bit as hot as his burning face and hands. How could he relax when dying was the most appealing way for each passing nano-second to end? "I'm blind. I'm blind."

"It'll be okay," Beryl said.

"No it won't be, my eyes are gone, you stupid bitch." Manfred touched his cheeks, felt something sharp, more steel from the aerosol can.

"Take no notice, Beryl, he's in agony," Terry said. "He doesn't mean it."

"I fucking do," Manfred yelled. "One of you idiots did something wrong, and now…now I'm blind."

"The doctors will be able to help you," Beryl said.

Something touched his shoulder. Her comforting hand?

He retracted away from it. The stupid bastards he worked with had done this. They were incompetent and inept. Barely a bloody brain cell between them. And here he was, the one with the chemistry degree, lying on the floor in seven shades of Hell.

I'll make them pay for this. Give them each their own version of Hell.

The heat had travelled bone-deep, seeming to hang on his cheekbones, around his jaw, and spear into his teeth. His throat hurt so much, and was tight, too, as if swollen.

Still he stared unseeing at the darkness. Not even a flicker of light or a shadow. Just absolute blackness. The type of black in deepest space. Nothing there.

And the dark was terrifying, almost as bad as the pain. Almost. His wails reduced to whimpers; he didn't have the strength to keep up the screaming. It was as if a plug had been pulled on his energy. He was slipping downwards, a spiral of fire and brimstone sucking him inwards.

"Shit, is he dying?" Terry.

"Damn it, where's the ambulance?"

Manfred quivered—it started in his heart and wended outward. Breathing was even more difficult now, the reduced space in his throat allowing only a ribbon of air to pass on each inhale and exhale. He was floating, disconnecting from the world as he knew it. The scientist in him wondered if that was nature's way, if his body was taking him from the pain by reducing his oxygen, helping him to go gently into the next world.

I take it all back. I do believe in God. I'm sorry for all the things I said about You. I do believe.

He reckoned a quick plea for forgiveness couldn't do any harm right now. He'd hedge his bets on the Big Bloke.

"The ambulance is here!" Fredrick's voice. Distant.

"Tell them to hurry," Beryl shouted. "He's in a bad way."

No shit, Sherlock.

"Hey, fellas, over here."

"Where is he?"

"This way."

Urgent, deep voices. Rapid footsteps.

"What's his name?"

"Mannie. It's Mannie."

Manfred tried to move his lips to correct him, but they were puffing up, balloon-like.

"It's okay, mate, we're the paramedics. We're going to give you something to make you comfortable then get you to hospital. The doctors will sort you out."

"Yeah, you'll be right as rain in no time," Beryl added, then, "won't he?"

"Please, madam, if you could just move out of the way, let us do our job."

Manfred succumbed to the shallow breaths his lungs were insisting upon—the hangman's burn in his throat was excruciating and the blackness a cloak of terror wrapping tighter around his brain.

"Just a little scratch."

Something on his arm, nothing of note, and then the blackness thickened, and he slipped away from the voices and the heat in his skin.

"This will make him more comfortable."

"Good, because it's terrible, so terrible. One minute he was laughing and joking with us, working away, the usual, and then there he was, flat on his back, on fire...his face melted."

Melted.

The last word Terry had spoken rattled around Manfred's brain. It ricocheted, pinging around, gathering speed, a bullet in a barrel.

Melted

Melted

Melted

A wax dummy standing too close to the fire. A candle burning down to the wick. Was that how his life was going to end? It seemed so undignified, so unbecoming.

He mumbled, his lips not seeming to move, then with relief the pain receded. He knew it hadn't really gone away. He understood that. They'd given him a potent chemical, most likely an opioid, morphine, which would attach to the receptors that transmit pain messages to the brain.

He'd never been so thankful for the opium poppy, papaver somniferum, in his life.

"That's it, you can rest, we've got you."

The voices were even farther away now. Manfred didn't even bother to try to answer. Breathing was difficult, hell, he wasn't even sure if he could be bothered to do that.

And as he slipped away, to blissful oblivion, the last thought in his mind was of the barmaid at The Hanged Carpenter, her lush big boobs and bright smile.

Will she come to my funeral?

Chapter Two

Shona stared up at Earle as he stared down at her. Her pulse thudded in her ears, and her heart squeezed tighter with every contraction.

The lineup viewing room was silent but for their breathing, though her last words to Earle—"Thank you for being here, thank you for being you."—seemed to echo around the walls.

"That's the nicest compliment I've had in a long while," Earle said eventually.

"Ah, shut up." She gave him a gentle shove on his chest and tried to release some of the tension in hers. "You get compliments all the time. What about Short-shorts Lady yesterday, I can't remember her name...oh...yes... Tammy."

"Tammy isn't my new DI, you are, which makes the compliment quite different." He stepped away and shoved his hands into his pockets. "And for the record, I really appreciate you trusting me enough to tell me all of this."

"I didn't want to. What I mean is I wish...I wish it wasn't there to be told."

"I get that." He paused.

She felt she needed to elaborate. "I was...*am* a victim." She gestured down herself. "What happened to Lina happened to me, only I wasn't so lucky. No one took me to safety, no one looked after me when I couldn't look out for myself."

"You survived."

She glanced away. Yes, she'd been the lucky one, had found the strength to carry on, and used her need for revenge to bolster her determination to get well and find the culprits. That hadn't happened for Nicola and Tina. They'd crumpled, been destroyed by that night.

"I've got to get out of here," she said, suddenly feeling as if the walls were closing in. "It makes me sick to know he was so close to getting thrown behind bars, for a while at least, but now he's free and just gone about his business." She pointed at the entrance to the lineup room. "Out there in Ironash."

"Driving a van. That's his business during the day." Earle spread out his fingers then drew them into fists. "A van we can keep a close eye on."

"Yes, so let's go and do some digging."

Shona stepped up to the door, but before she opened it, Earle spoke again.

"Be positive. This time yesterday you didn't even have a name, right?"

She thought back to standing in Frasers sniffing aftershaves to see if one triggered more memories. It had been a futile exercise. She now knew the scent she was searching came from cooking with spices. "Yes, you're right. I have a lot more now. Trouble is, it's made me impatient, I'm itching for the arrest. It's been a long wait."

"The perfect arrest is like baking the perfect soufflé."

"What?" She turned to him.

He shrugged, his wide shoulders lifting and falling beneath his crisp white shirt. "Sometimes the damn thing won't rise, no matter what you do, but every now and again it rises and it's appearance is award-winning and it tastes better than you ever could have dreamed it would." He grinned, flashing his perfect white teeth. "One arrest would have been great, three is going to be even better. It's worth biding your time for the big prize."

"God, I hope you're right."

"We can only try, and with two brains being better—"

"Okay, enough with the analogies, lets get a coffee, the last one went cold."

He chuckled. "Good plan."

After fixing the coffee situation, and with Fletcher, their DCI, in his office with the door closed, Shona dug into her drawer.

"Take a gander at this." She pulled out the sketch Barry Grey, the police artist, had created from her description of Samri Laghari.

"Bloody hell." Earle pressed his palm on the desk, elbow straight, and stared down at it. "That's a pretty damning likeness."

"A bit younger perhaps, but he's got some unique features."

"And they've been captured perfectly." He nodded. "He's very talented, Barry."

"One of the best I've come across."

"And you remembered all of this detail? It was what…eight years ago?"

"Not exactly from current memory."

Earle frowned.

Shona sighed and plonked down in her chair. It was a spinning one, so she twisted from side to side. It was weird to be talking so openly about a subject she'd kept such a shield around. "I went to see a hypnotist."

He waited for her to go on.

"She dragged some memories from me."

"That can't have been easy."

"No, it was pretty traumatic, same way as being so close to him yesterday was." She suppressed a shudder. "But you saw Lina for yourself. Once a roofie is in your system, that's it." She made an explosion signal over her head. "Everything is gone, your mind is a blank, nothing. And nothing was no good to me. I needed something."

"Well, you certainly got it."

"Not enough to convict, though."

"But enough to get us to this point, and from here we can do what we're paid to do, investigate." He rolled up the sketch and passed it to her. "Where do you want me to start?"

"I'll send you the case file?" She tucked the sketch in her drawer.

"You sure?" He raised his eyebrows.

"It's personal, yeah, but you're a professional." She glanced around at the other officers in the room, junior and more senior. "But let's keep it between us for now, is that okay?"

"Goes without saying. Andy isn't in anyway, not today, and he's the one to pass the tech things on to."

"Oh yes, it's his step father's funeral, right?"

"I believe so."

She tutted. "And we kept him on the go until late into the night. I feel bad about that, but blimey, we needed him."

"I've known Andy a while. Working last night will have kept his mind off things. A welcome relief. Sometimes its good to have distraction, don't you agree?"

"Yes, I do." She thought of the last eight years rising to DI. "It gives you something else to focus on."

"Exactly."

He smiled and pointed at his computer. "Send me that file. I'll get up to speed."

"Thanks." She sipped her coffee. "And I'll start digging into Samri's world."

She set her attention on her screen and began to delve into the life of her attacker. It wasn't somewhere she wanted to go, but she had no choice. Not if she was to finally find closure.

His white van was a ten-year old Ford diesel, the registration number noted. He had one speeding ticket, just about to expire on his licence. His address was at the opposite end of Ironash to hers—thank goodness for small mercies.

Was I taken to his home?

Shona had no idea.

Because he'd been held on reasonable suspicion of attempting to commit an offence, his fingerprints had been taken on arrival at the police station the night before. Shona drew up his rap sheet. It was empty—this was his first visit to the home of the law.

"Too bloody clever," she muttered. "Keeps getting away with it."

"What?" Earle said.

"Nothing."

She sighed, wrote *Other DR Cases* on a Post-it note, then moved on to social media to glean what she could about Samri Laghari.

But she quickly drew a blank. His name, or variations of it, didn't appear on Facebook, Twitter, or Instagram. A Google search had one mention of him being available as a man with a van, but that information was from three years ago and was buried in a hundred adverts for local gardeners, decorators, and plumbers.

She sighed, a long expulsion of air that ended on a groan.

"You okay?" Earle asked.

"I was hoping to find something on social media, but nothing. No web presence."

"Don't stress it. Andy will look when he's back, that's his thing."

"But how hard can it be?"

"What can I say, it's like Andy has a magic wand."

Shona finished her coffee and tamped down her frustration. "Remind me again how many CCTV cameras there are in Ironash town centre?"

"Eight in total plus a few privately owned ones."

"And I know one is outside REVS."

"Yeah." He frowned. "So how come...?"

"It wasn't working. The only witness to us leaving with three men was a bouncer who was busy dealing with a situation and his account was flaky at best. The camera drew a blank, literally."

"Damn." He nodded at the phone. "I'm going to get all the council ones checked, what do you think?"

"A damn good idea. If Samri had a go at slipping a roofie last night, it means he's got a supply and is brewing for a hit. Bastard. We need our bases covered."

Earle paused, his jaw tense. "You really think he'll strike soon?"

"Why not? Like I said, I always presume the worst. Which reminds me, I need to study those other local date-rape cases."

"I believe there's six others. Do you need a hand finding them?"

"No, I'm okay with this system. You check on those cameras."

Shona drew up the file cases she was looking for. Since she'd arrived at Ironash she'd been meaning to study them, hunt for more clues and find similarities with her case. But between Roy Campbell and Olga Umbridge, she'd barely had a moment to sit at her desk, let alone concentrate on a bunch of evidence, data, and facts.

The first was a year to the day of her attack. She had to check twice. Coincidence? Again it had been three young women drugged, taken, and dumped. Not from REVS this time, but from a wine bar—Grapes Ahoy—at the far end of High Street. The two witnesses were unreliable due to intoxication, their stories changing multiple times upon questioning. The girls all showed signs of sexual contact, restraint and urine samples revealed traces of rohypnol.

Shona flicked through the evidence photographs. A rise of bile flooded her gullet, and she swallowed, massaging her throat. The images were harrowing, with rope marks around wrists, ankles, and necks. The scared, vacant, confused glint in each girls' eyes brought back a ton of memories of looking at herself in the the mirror those first months—of seeing Nicola and Tina never lose that terror.

The drop-off location was the same, Six Mile Lane. Naked and scrubbed clean, scared, and memories erased.

She made a few notes, documented names and ages, then went to the next file.

The same whirlwind of emotions raged through her. She scratched her head with the pen and fiddled with the button on her blouse. Jotted a few details down.

By the time she was onto the next case, frustration was mounting. There was absolutely no evidence. After the DNA found in her case, under Nicola's fingernails, Samri and his two friends—because she presumed this was a threesome gang as it was always three women taken—had been very careful. The women were spotless.

She read through the victim accounts. REVS seemed to be the most popular pickup spot for Samri's gang. But there wasn't much to go on. Once the drug had taken hold, memories were scant. Two woman mentioned a dark-haired man with broad shoulders—could be Samri. And two mentioned a thinner man with a long face and dull blond hair, which Shona suspected was the other bloke she'd seen while under hypnosis.

The sooner I get his sketch done the better.

She set to work on the last file. A kernel of hope still lived. Perhaps there'd be more to go on in here.

But no. Another attack on three girls and nothing for the Ironash police to work with. These vile men had their evil deeds fine-tuned. What was worse was they treated it like an annual party. July was strike time. Like clockwork, that was when they hit.

"And this year I'll be waiting."

"What?" Earle said again.

"Er, nothing." She leaned back, stretched, and rubbed her stomach. "I'm getting hungry."

"No wonder, it's gone two. Why don't I wander to Greggs, get us something?"

"Good idea, I'll come with you. I could do with the walk." She stood, nodding at Fletcher's still-closed door. "Do you think he'll want something?"

"We'll grab him a Steak Bake, he'll sulk if we don't."

They headed out into what was proving to be another warm and muggy day, though there were a few heavy gunmetal-grey clouds gathering on the horizon.

"Maybe we'll get a storm," Earle said, setting off at his usual ground-eating pace.

"That would clear the air at least, give the garden a water. Lawn needs it." God, she sounded like her mother, and she'd only been home a few weeks.

Earle didn't reply.

They rounded the corner housing Blighty Bingo and walked towards Haymarket. There were people milling about—mothers with prams, dog walkers, shoppers, and two blokes were unloading a white van into an antique shop.

Shona automatically scanned the registration plate.

No, not Samri's.

She took a deep breath. "So what did you make of my case file?"

Earle scratched his temple. "I just have to say I'm really sorry you—"

"Please, don't say it. I know you are, you're a good bloke, Earle. I know you wouldn't wish what happened to me and my friends on anyone."

"Too damn right I wouldn't." He cleared his throat. "But we'll get them, we will."

"This is the closest I've ever been."

Gregg's blue sign appeared in the distance, after a Guide Dogs For the Blind charity shop.

"We need to do another full search on the DNA in your case, the suspect may be on the system now."

"Yes. We also need to speak to security at REVS and Grapes Ahoy. They need to be aware what's been going on. We need them on side."

"Have you been back there since...?"

"No. But I know I'll have to."

"We'll face that together."

"Thanks." She paused. Damn, it was good to have a wingman. "Hey, isn't that Andy?" Shona recognised the young man striding towards them in a black suit and tie.

"Yeah. It is."

They drew closer.

Andy spotted them and stopped.

"I thought you were at a funeral?" Earle said.

"I was, have been, it was early, ten-thirty." He gestured over his shoulder with his thumb. "My entire family are holed up in The Hanged Carpenter right now. They're all several sherries in and hashing out old squabbles." He tutted and poked a finger into his ear. "My mother has five sisters; the volume level is reaching pneumatic drill levels."

"But why aren't you there?" Shona said, glancing from Andy to the sign for the pub. She'd always thought it gruesome the way the carpenter had been painted swinging from a noose, his legs dangling above the ground and his face a horrid puce colour, fat tongue lolling to one side.

"I'm sorry to say it, ma'am, but I can't stand it. The noise, the bickering. I've shown my face, they don't need me. I pleaded an urgent case and made my excuses. I'll sit with my mother later, when they all go home."

Both Earle and Shona were silent.

"I'm sure there's something I can be doing, right?" There was a pleading tone in Andy's voice.

"There's always something for you to do." Shona smiled. "Want anything from Greggs?"

"No, I've had enough sausage rolls and mini quiche to last a lifetime." He stepped around them. "I'll see you at the station. Throw your worst at me."

"Yeah, see you in a few." Earle held up his hand as Andy turned and strode away.

"The worst," Shona said. "We might just do that."

Chapter Three

"Alexa, lights on."

Manfred had no idea if his electronic assistant had done what he'd asked. But if he didn't trust her, what good was she?

Yes, of course it's a her, she's got a girl's voice.

He wouldn't bother with lights at all, what was the point? But Marmaduke needed to see. And Marmaduke was essential—or Duke as he'd been known since coming from puppy training. Duke's canine eyes did the seeing for Manfred. That was how it had been for the last eighteen months, blind as a bat. Nothing. Nada. Zilch. Not even a flicker of light, a shadow or a single flash of colour.

That damn aerosol had exploded and turned each eyeball into a mushy, useless mess.

Which pissed the hell out of him.

But then on other days he thought it was just as well he couldn't see. His face was a right state—it felt as though someone had grated his skin off then slapped it back on higgledy-piggledy. His lips were wonky, he could feel that when he spoke or attempted a rare smile. His nose, which had always been on the large size, had a big dent on the end, and the septum was askew. He'd once had a full head of hair, been proud of a hairline that hadn't heard of the word receding, but that wasn't the case now. Now he had to put sunscreen on his bald brow and all around his ears if there was even a hint of a warm day.

A rumble of thunder sounded in the distance—a long grumble that competed with his tinnitus. Had the noise been accompanied by a lightning flash?

"There, there, you're safe in here, Duke." Manfred reached down, found his dog's head, and rubbed it. "Let's close the curtains so you'll feel better."

Moving carefully across the kitchen, he drew the curtains. He could picture them in his mind—they were blue with white polka dots on them. A jolly pattern, he'd told himself when he'd bought them three years ago. Little had he known then that patterns and colours would soon be so insignificant in his life, along with beautiful women, stunning views, and classic artwork.

"Alexa, play Mozart's *Requiem*." The constant ringing in his ears bugged him. Music was a good distraction.

"Playing *Requiem*, by Wolfgang Amadeus Mozart."

The haunting introduction filled the room, the gentle violin melody lulling the unwitting listener into a false sense of security of what was to come. And then it hit. Wild and feral, the battle to end all battles, the destruction of the universe. An operatic voice with passion and heat, electric hunger, determination, and fervour.

The hairs on the back of Manfred's neck stood up as he reached into the fridge and withdrew two fillets of salmon. He set them on the table, then returned to the fridge. For a moment he pretended to be the conductor, waving his arms around to the frantic tune.

Until his right hand bashed the fridge door and a sharp pain shot up to his elbow. "Ah fuck."

Manfred barked, once.

"Shit that hurt, stupid bloody fridge." He closed the door, a real hard slam. The contents shook, the milk rattling off a bottle of white wine.

Frowning, he rubbed his scarred hand then reopened the fridge. He had a meal to prepare. But not a boring old lasagne, or cottage pie for one, not tonight. Oh no. Tonight he had company. In fact, he had several dinner dates planned for the next week.

If he could pick anyone to join him for dinner it would be that Carol from the weather on TV. Whenever Manfred heard her voice, he remembered her boobs—a perfect handful and always in a slightly too-tight top. But sadly it wasn't Carol, it was that tosser, Terry, coming to tea.

They were always willing to pop round, the Fucking Useless Four, to spend time with him. They wanted to make sure he wasn't lonely, Beryl had once said.

What am I, a goddamn charity case?

But he let them visit. Forked out for the food and wine, too. He'd rather that. Was better than going to The Hanged Carpenter and imagining the pity-filled looks his old dart mates gave him, or heaven forbid, what the barmaid, his once-crush, thought now. Likely she'd have to press her hands to her mouth to stop herself vomiting when he and Duke walked in. Manfred had never been an oil painting, but at least back then he hadn't been a monster.

The music reached a crescendo as another roll of thunder vibrated through the house.

Duke whined.

"There, there, old boy." He sought a treat from an old biscuit tin. "Have this, take your mind off the noise."

Manfred felt his way to the oven and turned it on. It was specially adapted and clicked so he knew what temperature it was at.

He then sought a bag of frozen chips from the freezer and a packet of petits pois.

Once upon a time, when these damn dinners with the Fucking Useless Four had started, he'd hoped they'd bring a takeaway round, save a poor old blind man having to cook.

But now he was glad that routine had never started. And when Fredrick had mentioned it once, he'd said he liked to cook, it was something he could still do even though it took him a little longer.

It had been that moment his plan had been germinated. And ever since it had been growing, peeking from the depths of his mind like a sapling from the earth, forming a weak limb at first, but then branches, four of them, each filled with leaves and fruit.

Forbidden fruit.

A good hollandaise sauce, now that was something Manfred loved. Always had.

He felt around the counter for the eggs, cracked two into a bowl, then set about gathering white vinegar—he hoped it was the white—butter, and a Jif lemon.

As Duke crunched on his treat, Manfred made the sauce. He'd become used to checking the texture of his culinary creations with the slide of the spoon, and this one seemed okay.

The music came to an end.

"Alexa, what is 'digoxin'?"

"The noun 'digoxin' is usually defined as the cardiovascular drug digitalis derived from the plant leaves of digitalis and widely used in the treatment of heart failure."

He chuckled. She had a go, bless her, and was almost right. It also amused him that so many people walked past an innocent-looking foxglove, admiring its beauty, without knowing that within it was one of the most potent chemicals used to treat heart arrhythmias. Slow, steady, strengthen, that was what it did, that foxglove.

In the right doses.

But if you took too much...

With the sauce perfect, Manfred located his pestle and mortar.

"Alexa, play John Williams' *Jaws*."

"Playing *Jaws* by John Williams on Spotify."

The familiar *duh-du, duh-du* started up, its drumbeat rising Manfred's heart rate and sending a tingle down his spine.

"Alexa, volume up."

It turned up a notch, and Manfred grinned, his lips stretching in a way they never used to. "Tonight is the night." He imagined himself as a huge unstoppable shark, sliding through the water, searching out his prey, his instincts finely tuned and his cunning like no other.

"You should have stayed out of the water," he said, then cackled and reached for his medicine stash.

He rifled through what was a substantial amount of drugs, then located, using the braille on the front of the box, the digoxin. "Come to Daddy. Oh yes, come to Daddy."

He whistled to the music, anticipation tightening his belly. He hoped he'd be able to eat his dinner okay.

Tapping over the surface, he found his pestle and mortar, a gift Fredrick had brought him back from Crete once. Ironic now, wasn't it, what it was going to be used for.

The mortar was clean and silky smooth and the pestle satisfyingly heavy—it would take a chunk out of a skull, that was for sure. But violence wasn't his thing. He preferred a more subtle approach to his mission.

He popped eight tablets from the blister pack into the mortar. This totalled two milligrams, eight times more than the dose he used to steady his heart rate. A whopping dose, one that any cardiac muscle would struggle to cope with.

Duh, duh. Duh, duh. Duh, duh.

Jaws was closing in, getting nearer to its victim who was splashing around happily as if there were no danger to fear. Completely oblivious.

Manfred began to crush the tiny tablets, humming while he worked. He couldn't remember being so excited about something. At least not since his accident. This really was a fucking good laugh.

When he was satisfied there was only fine powder in the mortar, he added it to the hollandaise sauce and whisked it through. After dipping his thumb and index finger in and feeling for grit—there was none—Manfred was happy that his creation was perfect.

"Alexa, music off."

Jaws was silenced.

"Alexa, what time is it?"

"The time is seven 'o' five p.m."

Great, that gave him twenty-five minutes to tidy up, feed Duke, and switch the porch light on. It would be darkening outside, what with the storm. Made no difference to him, but he liked to be considerate, or at least give the illusion of that.

Soon the doorbell chimed, and Manfred answered it, feeling up from the door handle for the latch. As he opened, the sound of the rain hitting the pavement whooshed around him.

Duke pushed against him, sniffing the air.

"Hey, Mannie, how are you doing?"

"Terry, great to...hear you." He managed a smile, more of a grimace really, but Terry wouldn't take offence at that.

"Ha, glad you still have a sense of humour." Terry slapped him on the shoulder. "I brought red, is that okay?"

"We're having fish, but I don't suppose it matters."

"Nah, not exactly connoisseurs, are we?"

Maybe you would be if you knew this was your last supper.

Manfred stepped to one side so Terry could pass, then shut the door.

"Bloody awful out there," Terry said. The scent of the storm had followed him in. "Good job I had my brolly."

"Did you walk?"

"Yeah, thought I might as well, so we can have a few drinks together and all that."

"Good, I'm pleased." Duke was beside Manfred's legs, no doubt sniffing Terry's feet.

"Hey, Duke, how are you doing?"

Duke's wagging tail hit Manfred. That bugged him. Duke was supposed to have some loyalty, not be friends with one of the idiots who'd ruined his life.

He doesn't understand.

Manfred gestured towards the kitchen. "Shall we? Duke hates this weather. He's best off in his bed beside the radiator."

"Yeah, of course."

When they reached the kitchen, Terry spoke again. "Want me to do anything?"

"You could open that wine."

"Ah, that I can do."

Manfred put the fish and the chips in the oven. He set the peas to boil.

"Shall I pour?" Terry asked.

"Yes, glasses are on the table." Manfred had given up on his small dining room since the accident. It was easier to use one room for preparing food and eating, less stumbling about with plates full of food.

"Of course."

Glug. Glug. Glug.

Excellent. Nice generous glasses suited Manfred. Less chance of Terry noticing anything was amiss.

"Here."

Manfred was aware of Terry's close proximity, of a glass of wine being pressed into his hand.

"Have a sip of this."

"Cheers." Manfred took a slug. "Mmm, it's good. French?"

Terry guffawed. "Shit, man, you are a connoisseur. How'd you know?"

"Lucky guess."

"Nah, I read that when you lose your sight your other senses become heightened. Maybe that's your next career, a wine bloke. What are they called...?"

"Sommelier."

"Yeah, that's the one. New career for you and all that."

"With my ugly mug? I don't think so." Manfred jolted forward when a slap landed on his shoulder.

"Don't be so hard on yourself, you're okay. Probably feels worse than it actually is."

He huffed. He knew damn well he resembled a zombie having a bad hair day. He could hear it in people's voices, the shock, the fascination, the hesitancy, when they met him for the first time. Sometimes people even spoke to him as if his goddamn brain had melted in the accident. Might have been better if it had.

"Dinner won't be long. Fish, chips, and peas with a homemade hollandaise sauce."

"Sounds yummy, bring it on." Terry moved away—the chair legs scraped on the floor. "So tell me, what have you been up to since I last saw you?"

Fuck all. My life is over thanks to you. "Oh, this and that, you know, hanging out, listening to my music, enjoying the odd Scotch."

"Oh, I'll have one of them later."

"Of course, if you still fancy one after..."

"After?"

Manfred smiled. "After dinner. Hollandaise can be a bit heavy."

"Ah, it'll be good for the digestion." Terry chuckled.

Manfred could just imagine him rubbing his potbelly, his shirt no doubt straining at the buttons and allowing unsavoury pale flesh to peek through. He pressed his lips together, the right side of his mouth flattening harder than the left. He decided it best to keep quiet about the fact that if Terry did ever get to that tipple, it would be a bloody miracle.

Chapter Four

Shona and Earle wandered back to the station, munching a sausage roll each. Tiny flakes of pastry fluttered in their wake, and when she'd finished, Shona instantly regretted the grease coating her mouth.

"Mmm, these are good." Earle started on his second sausage roll—a step too far for Shona.

"Hello, ma'am, sir." Darren looked up from his screens on the reception desk and nodded at them as they walked past.

"Hey, Darren," Shona said. "Anything going on we need to know about?"

"No, all calm, which to be honest, we deserve after this last week."

"No kidding." She brushed a crumb from her blouse. "The festival packed up yet?"

"More or less."

"Good." She downturned her mouth. "I wonder if they'll even run it next year, after the Umbridge case."

"It would save us a lot of hassle if they didn't." Darren shrugged. "But I guess we'll have to wait and see." The reception landline phone rang, and he picked it up.

Shona and Earle went up to the main office.

Andy was sitting at his desk, his three screens lit up. He'd loosened his black tie and ran his hand through his hair, making it stick up at an angle.

"Shall we get him started on Samri Laghari?" Earle asked Shona quietly.

"No time like the present."

"Want me to..."

"Ask him without giving too much away? Yes, please." Shona smiled up gratefully. "Thanks."

Earle shrugged and stopped at Andy's desk. "We had a guy in, Samri Laghari."

"Okay." Andy nodded. "Go on."

"We suspect him of being involved in the date-rape cases."

"Ah, yeah, the ones that roll around each summer."

Shona's heart squeezed, and she suppressed a lurching nausea—the last thing she needed was her Greggs making a reappearance.

"That's it, the cases that always draw a blank." He glanced at Shona. "We think we might be able to make a breakthrough."

"But you need evidence, details, his online life." Andy picked up a pen. "How is he spelling his name?"

Earle spelt it out.

Andy wrote it down. "Good, that's nice and unusual. John Smith is the worst. Samri Laghari, there can't be too many of them around. I'll do some digging."

"Thanks." Earle clasped his shoulder. "But if you need to go back to your family…"

"I'll have to at some point, but believe me, this is a better place to be than The Hanged Carpenter right now."

Shona walked to her desk and sat while Earle got them both a coffee. When he set a steaming mug down, she was onto forensics. "I'll request another check on the DNA from my case, see if there's a match now."

"Good idea."

Shona set to requesting a DNA evidence updated check, and then began rereading the files on the other cases. It was what Andy had said that was bugging her, not that she hadn't had the same thought, but this annual date-rape event in Ironash. What was it about July? And what else linked the three men?

Samir Laghari, her attacker.

The blond man with the hooked nose and large ears she'd seen when under hypnosis—the man who'd hurt Tina's mind so bad she'd been in a psychiatric hospital for the last few years.

Vince, surname and description unknown, was also a murderer as far as Shona was concerned.

She scrolled through rap sheets, looking at faces, searching for clues.

Nothing.

"DI Williams, DS Montague, can I speak with you both?" Fletcher stood at his office door, one hand on the frame.

"Certainly." She stood.

Earle followed her in, closing the door behind him.

"Please, sit." Fletcher pointed at two chairs.

He wore a serious expression. Obviously something was bothering him.

"We've had two serial killers in Ironash which makes me very uncomfortable." Fletcher scratched his head. "And it has put us on the radar for the serious crime squad."

"We solved both cases, sir," Shona said.

"And with remarkable speed. I'm impressed." He gave a weak smile. "Though it would be better not to have dead bodies on our hands at all."

"I agree." Earle crossed his legs, his polished shoe bobbing in the air as though stabbing it. "Young or old, they shouldn't have had their lives stolen like that."

"Absolutely."

"What's worrying you?" Shona asked.

"I know you're new to the Ironash detective team," Fletcher said, "but each year, around this time, young girls have been targeted in alarmingly similar date-rape cases."

Shona swallowed.

He set his attention on her. His piercing blue eyes were unblinking. She held his gaze.

"But you know that, right?" he said.

She clenched her jaw so hard she worried her teeth might break. "Yes, sir."

He knows. He's not stupid. He's seen my file.

"And this year." He tilted his chin, his attention on her unwavering. "I do not want a repeat of innocent young girls being preyed upon."

She pressed her lips together, waiting for him to reveal he knew she'd been a victim. That she'd been drugged, taken, and molested.

"It's why we were quick to act at the festival, sir," Earle said, "when we saw someone who matched the description of a suspect."

Shona resisted the urge to look at Earle. Instead, she knotted her fingers on her lap and stared at a photograph of Fletcher receiving an award.

"It was a vague description and an unsuccessful lineup." Fletcher tutted.

"Yes, sir." Earle nodded. "It was."

"But..." Fletcher leaned forward, elbows on his desk, fingertips steepled. "DI Williams, you've settled in fast. It's clear you and DS Montague make a good team. I'd like you to focus entirely on these past cases and make sure we don't have a repeat this year."

She cleared her throat. "Yes, sir. Of course."

His focus on her was penetrating, as if he could see into her soul.

He knows. He knows.

Earle's foot continued to bob, faster now.

"I suspect it's the same perpetrators," Fletcher said, "like your common house burglar who figures out a mode of entry and sticks to it, that's what these scumbags are doing. Drug, attack, then get rid of all evidence."

Shona swallowed again and glanced at Earle.

He was staring straight ahead, a tendon jumping in his cheek.

"Put everything into it once you're up to date on paperwork." Fletcher nodded at the door. "And use Darren and Andy as much as you need. I'm thinking we have a small window of attack here if history repeats itself. Why that's the case, I have no idea."

"Yes, sir. We will." Shona nodded. "Concentrate our efforts, that is." She rolled her shoulders, trying to rid the itchy feeling she always got when her victim status was revealed, no matter how covertly Fletcher was doing it.

Strictly speaking she shouldn't be working on a case she was directly involved in, but these files were stacking up year on year, with no progress, perhaps that was why Fletcher was turning a blind eye.

For now.

"Good. It would be nice to get this string of particularly unpleasant cases wrapped up and these lowlifes behind bars."

Shona nodded, not quite trusting herself to speak now.

Earle stood. "Is that all, sir?"

"Er...not quite. I need to speak to you, DS Montague."

"Am I in trouble?" He raised his eyebrows.

"No, of course not."

Earle gestured to Shona. "Then just say it. Partners don't have secrets."

Fletcher pulled in a breath. He moved his attention from Shona to Earle. "I'm afraid there was a shooting last night, in Manchester."

"Manchester?" Earle stretched the word out. "And...?" He folded his arms, rocked back on his heels.

"And it involved Patrick."

The air in the room seemed to still.

Earle froze. "*My* Patrick?"

"Yes, your ex-partner."

"Is he...?"

"No, he's not dead. But he did take two bullets."

"Two. Shit." Earle sat with a bump and gripped the arms of the chair. "And he's okay...?"

"His vest took one, his right arm the other. He'll have an impressive scar, but I've been assured he'll live to tell the tale." Fletcher rubbed his chin. "I thought you'd want to know, Earle."

"Yes, of course. I'll...drop him a message." Earle stood again, paced left and then right. "Shit. I knew he was going somewhere...like that...but..."

"It's inner city policework, the risks are greater," Shona said. "Bullets have a habit of flying between gangs, and if you get caught up, you get hit."

Earle turned to her.

She could have sworn that his dark skin had lightened a tone. "Are you okay?"

"Yeah, yeah...fine." He pointed at the door. "Are we done here?"

"Yes," Fletcher said. "And I'm sorry to be the bearer of bad news, I know you're close."

"Were." Earle shoved his hands in his trouser pockets. "We *were* close."

He strode from the room, his movement creating a breeze that lifted a few strands of Shona's hair.

"You got a handle on this?" Fletcher asked her.

"What? Earle or the date-rape cases?"

"Both."

She stood, pulled in a deep breath. "Of course, it's my job."

He smiled then picked up his phone. "You know where I am if you need me."

"Thank you, sir."

She left his office and took her seat next to Earle. "Have you messaged him?"

"No, not yet."

She paused. "He called, the other day, when we were in the car, right?"

He shrugged. "Yeah, and now I feel like a right bastard for not picking up."

"We were on a job. It's hardly been quiet around here."

He clicked his tongue on the roof of his mouth.

"Send him a message, let him know you care."

"Of course I care." There was a sharp tone to his voice.

Shona decided not to push it and returned her attention to her computer.

After a couple of minutes, Andy wandered over carrying a few sheets of paper.

"Anything?" Shona asked.

"The guy lives off grid. No Facebook, Instagram, Snapchat, or Twitter. I got a number for his phone, he's with O2. His recent calls are to local restaurants and shops and three to a number in Pakistan. I suspect he uses WhatsApp, but of course, that's encrypted, so I have no idea who he communicates with on there."

"Okay, good work. Anything else?"

"Drives a white Ford van, one speeding ticket. He lives on the Scooners Estate, which is the address he gave when brought in."

"Alone?"

"Not sure."

"Can you check?"

"Sure. And do you want me to organise someone to go round there, keep a watch on his movements?"

"No, that's not necessary at this point. As long as he's in town we can keep an eye on him." She paused. "Have you got enough cameras to do that?"

"Yeah, just about if he's in the centre, and we have ANPR."

She nodded, and the flicker of a thought tugged. "When you looked at his phone records, did he happen to call The Bay Leaf?"

"That's the Indian to the west of High Street, right?"

"Yes."

He checked his sheet of paper. "No, not in the last week."

"Mmm, okay, well, if he's spotted on CCTV with anyone else, take a still. I need to know who he's hanging out with."

"Yes, ma'am." He dipped his head, then walked away.

Shona sighed, wishing her frustration had huffed out on the long exhale. Sadly, it hadn't. Without social media, it was harder to see who Samri communicated with.

Her phone rang. She checked the screen.

Ben. Karate.

For a moment she thought about ignoring it, her head was in work mode, her nerves were twitchy, but then she hit answer. "Hey, Ben. Everything okay?"

"Yes, sorry to bother you."

"No problem." She was silent, waiting for him to speak.

"It's just that... I wondered..."

"Yes?"

"We've got an extra session tomorrow, at the dojo, a bunch of kids trying out for the first time. I could really do with a hand if you're free in the morning." He paused. "And then there's this nice little café, around the corner, I don't know if you've been, it's full of old books, and there's several cats there. They sit around, enjoying company."

She was silent. Cats?

"But if you're not a cat person, that's fine, too. It's just, I thought..." His voice trailed off.

"I'm not sure if I can, I've promised to spend some time with my parents, and..." But she did fancy helping out. Karate was good for her soul, rebalanced her thoughts, and put her mind and body in alignment. Lunch with Ben would hardly be torture. He was nice-looking, easy to chat to. Perhaps it was time for her to date.

Finally.

She tucked her hair behind her ears, tipped her head back, and closed her eyes.

"Oh, don't worry then," he said, "it was just me being silly, thinking maybe you'd be free, but of course you're very busy, what with your job and—"

"I'll let you know, okay. It depends on..."

"That's fine, let me know. Whenever." He took a deep breath. "No pressure, Shona."

She smiled. She liked the way he said her name. It was a nice change from ma'am and DI Williams. "I'll speak to you soon, bye."

"Goodbye, have a nice day."

She put her phone aside, only to find Andy standing next to her again.

He placed a grainy image on her desk. "I went through yesterday's footage on Bishop Street, picked up this."

"Bloody hell," she muttered.

"What?" Earle was also at her side.

She set her hand around her throat, her fingers digging into her flesh. Suddenly her breaths were shorter, her heart racing.

The man standing with Samri was the man she'd seen when under hypnosis. A long face, hooked nose, ears that meant he was likely nicknamed Dumbo at school. He was creepy, in a child-catcher kind of a way.

She pressed her finger beside his face. "I know him. I've seen him before."

Earle crouched so his face was level with hers. "Go on."

Her mouth had dried; her teeth hurt because of it. "He's one of them. One of the three."

Chapter Five

Manfred served up the salmon, using his sense of touch to ensure it was set in the middle of the plate.

"Smells great," Terry said from where he sat at the small Formica kitchen table. "Healthy, too. Doctor said I need to be a bit more health conscious, drop my blood pressure a notch and all that."

"Got to take care of your heart," Manfred placed the fish slice to one side. "You only get one ticker."

"And it's got to keep on ticking." Terry laughed then slurped his wine.

The rain pelted the window, or was it hailstones now? Duke whimpered.

"Would you do me a favour and give him a treat?" Manfred said, stirring the sauce. "He hates storms, poor thing."

"They're in the tin, right?"

"Yeah." Manfred decided it was worth the risk of tasting the hollandaise. He dipped the tip of a spoon in and set it on his tongue. He spread the silky liquid over the roof of his mouth. It was perfectly smooth and tasted great. Too bad he wouldn't have any.

"Here you go, mate. Munch on that."

Manfred ladled a big scoop of sauce onto Terry's dinner. He hoped it had covered the potatoes, and the broccoli, too, not that it mattered much. But it was, after all, a last meal, it should look good as well as taste good.

A rumble of thunder growled overhead. "Alexa, play chilled jazz."

"Playing chill-out jazz from Spotify."

The gentle tones of a lazy tune filled the room.

"That's better, will take Duke's mind off the thunder," Terry said.

Carefully, Manfred set Terry's dinner down, feeling for the edge of the table—he didn't want his hard work ending up on the floor. That would never do.

"Wow, this looks great," Terry said. "Well...sorry, you know, *smells* good, too."

"It's okay, I know you can see it and I can't." Manfred chuckled even though he hated Terry for being able to see, for not being the one maimed and disfigured that day.

But it's okay, revenge is only a few mouthfuls away.

He picked up his own plate and carefully sat opposite Terry.

"You not having any sauce?"

"No..." He'd prepared for this moment and rubbed his sternum. "Been having problems with heartburn lately. I'm better off sticking to bland stuff, at least that's what the doc said."

"Ah fuck, that's bad luck, you know, on top of everything else."

The sound of Terry shoving in food and chewing nosily travelled like nettle rash over Manfred's skin, heating him from the inside out.

"Luck seems to have evaded me this last couple of years."

"I know, sorry, mate. Still, there's plenty of time for it to pick up, eh."

"I guess."

More revolting chewing, the jazz did little to drown it out. Still, it would be over soon and worth it in the end.

Manfred started on his salmon. It really was very good.

"Gloria wants us to go to Greece in the summer," Terry said. "She wants blue sea, blue sky and all that."

"Sounds lovely."

"Crete is supposed to have the best views...you should go, Mannie."

Manfred said nothing and took a sip of wine.

"Well, shit, not for the views, obviously, you can't see them. But go for the food and wine. Damn, this really is good, you're an awesome bloody cook."

"I'm glad you like it. Is the sauce a bit thick?"

"No, it's perfect, better than any restaurant stuff." He chuckled. "Not that you'd get this at The Hanged Carpenter. Burger and chips, battered fish, lasagne, that's more their style."

"You been there lately?"

"A couple of weeks ago. Just for a pint." His cutlery scraped on the plate.

Manfred hoped that meant he was eating it all up like a good little murder victim. "Is that barmaid still there, the one with the big tits? What's her name again?"

"You mean Samantha? Yeah, she's still there. Not wearing her wedding ring these days, though."

Manfred pulled in a breath and released it slowly. If it wasn't for the Fucking Useless Four, he could have stepped into her husband's shoes and his side of the bed, he was sure of that. But Samantha hardly wanted his grotesque face to wake up to each morning—*who* would want that?

No one.

Duke came and sat next to him. Whimpered again.

"Wow, did you see that big flash?" Terry said.

"No."

"Shit, sorry, I'm really putting my stupid big foot in it tonight."

"It's okay."

"It's not, I am sorry. I suppose it's the storm, making me a bit twitchy, too." He cleared his throat. "Must be the sulphur in the air or something?"

"Are you okay?"

"Yes, fine." He coughed. "You want some more wine?"

"Yeah, go on, top me up." Manfred used his fingertips to locate the last of his dinner then speared it onto his fork. It had been tasty but would have been better with the hollandaise. He'd make himself some tomorrow, so he didn't feel like he'd missed out.

Another jazz tune came on, one he recognised—his mother used to play it. "How's work?"

"Oh, same old, same old. Darrell and Beryl have had a falling out."

"They have?"

"Yeah, Darrell made a comment about Beryl always farting, that it was giving him asthma or something." Terry laughed. "Beryl didn't take it well."

"No, I guess she wouldn't." Manfred pulled a face. "She does drop 'em, though."

"It's her condition, bad guts. That's why I got her those charcoal knickers for her secret Santa present last year."

"You didn't!"

"Yeah, I thought I told you." He laughed harder, but it ended on another cough. "That's why she didn't speak to me until March, but she didn't pong as much as usual, so maybe she was wearing them."

"Maybe." Manfred set his knife and fork down. "She's coming for dinner soon. I should cook something bland for both of us."

"Good idea." The chair legs scraped on the floor. "It's really hot in here?"

"Is it?" Duke moved from Manfred's side, as if following Terry. "I'm about right—temperature, that is."

"Phew, I'm not, got the right meat sweats on, and I didn't even have meat."

"Open a window if you want?"

"No, that's not fair on Duke." He paced the length of the kitchen, his footsteps clacking. "And it's raining hard."

Manfred recognised the tune of *Summertime* playing through Alexa. He sat back and folded his arms, jiggled his leg in time with the beat. There was nothing for him to do but sit and wait for the digoxin to take effect on Terry's cardiac muscle. It was kind of like a lazy summer's day. Wasn't like he could see the gloomy storm, was it?

"Fuck, I might just get a glass of water. Want one?"

"No, I'm good. Help yourself, though, you know where the glasses are."

The tap came on, went off. Noisy glugging.

"Any better?" Manfred asked.

"I suppose." Terry sat again with a bump. "Just feel a bit weird." He burped, long and loud. "Like my guts are cramping. Hope I'm not going to do a Beryl and start farting." He laughed, but the sound was strained.

"Fart away. I cope with Duke at it all the time." Manfred smiled then stood. "I've got some salted caramel ice cream. Want some?"

Terry groaned a little. "Probably shouldn't with this bellyache, but go on then."

Greedy bastard.

"Coming right up. Will cool you down if you're having a hot flush." He opened the freezer and located the ice cream from the top drawer.

"Hot flush. Cheeky bugger. I'm not some menopausal woman, you know."

You won't be anything soon.

More thunder.

Duke barked.

"It's okay, go in your bed." Manfred pointed to the corner of the room. "It will be over soon, Duke. All over."

As he scooped the ice cream into bowls, he wondered just how long it would take for the digoxin to throw Terry's heart into some kind of dysfunctional rhythm. He'd asked Alexa about it—she hadn't been very clear, but he remembered from his studies at uni that stomach cramps and visual disturbances were the first signs of acute toxicity.

"Here you go, Terry, sod the calories, right? We had a healthy dinner. Everything in life balances out in the end."

"Yeah, okay. Thanks."

Manfred sat. "Alexa, play *The End* by the Doors."

"*The End* by The Doors from Spotify."

They ate in silence as the song began calmly, with the singer bidding adieu to his friend.

"Bit depressing this," Terry said, scraping his spoon around the bowl.

"I like it. Rock classic, created from a bad trip."

"I feel like I'm having a bad trip." Terry laughed, stood and paced again. "My heart's pounding."

"Is it?" Manfred battled to keep the excitement from his voice. This was it, it was working, his longtime plan was coming to fruition.

"Yeah, like thudding, as if I've been running or something."

"Maybe it's the storm, like you said."

"Why would a storm…?" He paused and blew out a breath. "Bit dizzy, too."

"Tell you what," Manfred said. "You go and sit in the living room. I'll get us that Scotch each. Sort you out, that will."

"Yeah, I think I might." He set his hand on Manfred's shoulder. "But if it doesn't, I might have to cut our night short."

"That would be a shame." Manfred smiled, his lips twisting. It was one of the first genuine smiles in a while. "I look forward to our date nights."

"Date nights! Ha! You always were a laugh, Mannie."

He left the room.

Manfred quickly washed up the dinner plates and the saucepan the hollandaise had been in, then poured two glasses of Scotch. It really did feel like a celebratory drink. Damn shame he was blind, though. Watching Terry kick the bucket would have been fun.

He wandered into the living room, Duke at his side. He set the two drinks on the table between the sofa and his chair by the fireplace, then sat. "Feeling any better?"

"A bit." Terry swallowed. "I'll drink this and see."

"The best medicine."

Slurp.

Manfred smiled—he couldn't seem to stop smiling—and sipped his whisky.

For a few minutes they sat in silence. The storm rumbled on, as did Alexa in the kitchen, *The End* reaching its lyrical high, begging the listener to "ride the snake" and "ride the highway west." It really was a very good choice of song for this moment.

"Ah shit, I'm not good." Terry groaned. The sofa creaked as though he were rocking.

"What's up? What can I do?"

"I dunno…maybe call Gloria, she'll come and get me."

"Yes, of course." Manfred stood. He found Terry, squeezed his shoulder. "Hang on in there."

Terry groaned then coughed. "I don't think I could walk home feeling like this."

"And you probably shouldn't." He injected a healthy dose of concern into his voice.

Manfred went into the kitchen. He picked up his phone but didn't wake it. Instead, he spoke to a silent line. "Hi, Gloria, this is Manfred. Terry isn't feeling well. Do you think you could pick him up?" He paused. "Okay, that's great, see you in a few minutes." He set the phone to one side and went back into the living room. "How are you doing?"

"Not good at all. I feel like I'm suffocating. My breath…it's hard…to catch."

"Is your heart still pounding?"

"Yeah…g…going like the clappers." He moaned, and again the sofa creaked.

Duke barked, twice.

Manfred wondered if Terry had collapsed, so he dropped to his knees and felt around. He came into contact with Terry's leg, then his hip and the side of his body.

Yes, he was on his side. His breaths were shallow and jagged.

"Terry. What should I do?" Manfred asked. His own heart was thudding with excitement, fluttering against his sternum. The digoxin plan was working much better than anticipated.

"Amb...ambulance."

"Shit, yes, okay." Manfred jumped up, rushed to the kitchen, walloping his elbow on the doorframe.

He grabbed his phone and took it into the living room with it pressed to his ear. "Yes, ambulance please, 54 Drover Road. Hurry, I think my friend is having a heart attack." He placed the phone beside his whiskey. "Ambulance is on the way."

"Thanks...oh fuck..." Terry released a long strangled sound, as though he was suffocating, and then silence.

"Terry?" Manfred stood in the middle of the room, his face lifted to the ceiling as he listened for another breath.

The rain eased.

A weird stillness fell around him, like a velvet cloak covering his shoulders.

Even Duke was still and silent.

"Terry?"

Nothing.

He moved to the sofa, felt for Terry, found his face and held his hand beneath his nose. There was no movement of air. He set his hand on Terry's chest. It was still.

"You're dead," he said. "And it's what you deserved after what happened to me. Death would have been better than the life I have now, so think yourself lucky."

He stood, a wave of triumph going through him. He found his phone. This time he really did dial nine-nine-nine, using Siri, and asked for an ambulance. It was too late, of course it was. It would have been better to get Siri to dial up the undertaker, but there was a process to be gone through. It wouldn't do to create any suspicion around Terry the Dickhead's death.

"Alexa," he called towards the kitchen. "Play *Eye of the Tiger*."

"Playing *Eye of the Tiger* by Survivor from Spotify."

The first electric beats rang out. Manfred knocked back the last of his whisky, released an air punch, and whooped.

Chapter Six

"You really need to tell me everything," Earle said.

Shona glanced at Andy.

"I'll er..." Andy shifted from one foot to the other. "I'll go and keep digging."

"Yes, please, and run a biometric facial recognition scan, see if we can get a name on this new bloke," Shona said.

"On it." He walked away.

Earle pulled up his chair. He sat close to her with his forearms on his thighs, hands dangling between them. "You need to tell me everything, Shona. How do you know this man? I thought we were starting with nothing."

"We are, or rather, I was." She sighed. "But when I was under hypnosis last time he was there, in my memory. That man, I saw his face clear as day."

He was silent, waiting for her to go on.

"And he said something like, 'This bitch, Tina, she's mine. Stay the fuck away from her, Vince.'"

"Vince. So we have another name."

She nodded. "That's who he was talking to. But he, on CCTV, is the one who attacked Tina. At least that's what my buried memory tells me."

"And you're sure it's him? From that one picture?"

"Yes. As sure as I am Samri Laghari is guilty, and seeing them together, that just confirms it in my mind." She clenched her jaw, pointed at the small calendar on her desk. It had a picture of a butterfly on it. "And the fact that they're together, now, this week..."

"Means they're plotting." Earle stood and paced to the right. "Shit, we have to crack this case."

"I know." She looked at the picture again. There was something about the way the two men were leaning in close, talking covertly, that sent a shiver up her spine. She imagined their hushed whispers about evil deeds and disgusting plans. "We need to get their faces out to uniforms, bouncers, too. I need Andy and Darren watching High Street CCTV, especially in the evening, to see where they are, what they're doing. And if we spot them out and about, my God we need to follow them."

"Sounds like a plan."

"I've been planning this for a long time."

"I'm sure you have."

"Did you call Patrick?"

A flash seared over Earle's eyes, as if just the name being spoken out loud had affected him. "Yeah, I left a message."

She nodded. "He'll get back to you when he can."

Earle half shrugged. "Maybe." He set his hand on her shoulder, squeezed gently. "I'll chase up that DNA search, shall I?"

"Good idea." His touch was comforting. It told her he was on her side, that he was almost as determined as her to catch these bastards, even if he had other stuff going on in his personal life. She couldn't expect him to be *as* determined, because she was off the scale in her resolution to get justice. It would be served. She would have her moment.

Standing, she stretched out her spine, tipped her chin, and walked to the coffee machine. She poured two mugs, added a sugar to hers—she needed it—then went back to her desk. She set a drink down beside Earle.

"Wait," he said, reaching for a pen. He wrote on a pad of paper.

Vince Thomas.

"Vince?"

"Yeah, just in from forensics. Nicola's attacker now has a DNA profile. Seems he was a naughty boy eight months ago and got caught this time."

"Fuck, really?" She bit on her bottom lip. "It's a match? So we have a surname?"

"Yep, it is and we have."

"So why didn't he flag up when they took it?" A flush of anger and irritation pricked at her scalp.

"It was taken in Scotland."

"What?"

Earle shrugged. "Different forces, things slip though the net."

She tutted. "What did he do up in Scotland?"

"GBH charge, got off with a suspended sentence."

"I'm sure he has a long list of crimes. Must have been kicking himself to get caught and charged."

And murder is one of them—Nicola would still be alive if the scumbag hadn't used her for a night of his own sick pleasure.

"I reckon you're right." Earle sighed.

"Do we have an address?"

"A hostel in Glasgow. Chances of him still being there are slim to none."

"I agree."

"I'll give his name to Andy, add him to our digging list. We might get a more recent address."

"Good idea. Get an image of him, too, from the database. We need him watched out for like the other two."

"Will do."

She walked to the window and stared out. It wasn't quite as hot as it had been, and today there was no shimmer from the police station car park. Big fluffy white clouds were being gusted along by a gentle breeze. It would have been another nice day for festivalgoers, if the gig hadn't had to be shut down because of Olga Umbridge's killing spree.

She folded her arms, tight, hugging herself. The madness in Olga's eyes had given her the shivers. She'd seen something similar in Tina's eyes, last time she'd visited her on the psychiatric ward. As if she wasn't quite there. You could ring the doorbell, knock all you wanted, but there was no answer.

"Andy's on it." Earle was at her side.

"Thanks." She paused. "Did he mention…you know, me? Past cases?"

"His job isn't to dig into files, it's to dig into suspects."

She sighed. "Yes, I suppose."

"There's no shame in being a victim." He'd spoken quietly, his deep voice only just above a whisper. "It wasn't your fault."

Shona stared straight ahead, studying a small bird flitting around the branches of a tall oak. "Saying that and making it true are separate things, Earle." She tapped her fingers on her upper arms, a fast, tense movement. "And it's multi-layered, going from worthlessness, to guilt, to being embarrassed. There's so many what-ifs. What if I hadn't worn that outfit? What if we hadn't gone into the club? What if we hadn't left the drinks unattended? That's embarrassing in itself, that we did that. It was stupid."

"You have nothing to be embarrassed about."

She didn't speak. How could a big, confident bloke possibly understand what it was like to be female? When, for her, every taxi ride, lone trip with a man in a lift, date, could end in attack. Being female wasn't easy, it meant a life of being prey.

Which is why I'm a black belt now.

"Is there anything else?" Earle asked eventually. "From the hypnosis."

"Yes, actually there is." She moved back to her desk and pulled open the drawer. From it she retrieved the colourful sketch of the pattern she'd seen while under.

It was a bright-red circle, within it a square with gaps in the sides, four of them, like entrances into a maze. Then at the centre another circle. She'd coloured it in with yellow and orange, blue and green. "I saw this, very vividly, these colours, and it was big, huge, like a massive picture in an art gallery or something."

He took it and held it at arm's length.

"I don't know what it is or where the image came from." She shrugged. "It just did, it was there."

"It's a mandala."

Her jaw fell open, and her eyes widened. "A what?"

"A mandala."

"What on earth is that?"

"I don't know much about them, but it's a geometric design that holds a great deal of symbolism in Hindu and Buddhist cultures. I watched a program about Tibet a while ago. They were making them out of coloured sand, really intricate."

"I'll Google it." She plonked onto her chair and drew up Safari. "Here we go. A mandala is a spiritual and ritual symbol in Asian cultures. It can be understood in two different ways: externally as a visual representation of the universe or internally as a guide for several practices that take place in many Asian traditions, including meditation. In Hinduism and Buddhism, the belief is that by entering the mandala and proceeding towards its centre, you are guided through the cosmic process of transforming the universe from one of suffering into one of joy and happiness." She paused. "Bloody hell, why would I see that when I was being attacked?"

"I don't know, but you did, and judging by this picture, you saw it clearly."

Shona clicked on 'images', and a screen of different patterns jumped out at her. She scanned them quickly, looking for one that matched the bright colours of the one she'd seen. After a few minutes, she tutted in frustration.

"Go to shopping." Earle pointed to the top of the search screen.

Again the screen flicked over to a new set of images. Five down, a picture of a mandala, similar to hers in pattern but different in colour appeared. "Bingo." She jabbed at it with her finger. "This is a full size sheet, hung on a wall. That must be what I saw. That's why it's so big."

"We can run a check, find everyone who has bought one of these and see if there's a match for Ironash."

"We could." But even as she'd spoken her heart sank. There were so many sites selling similar mandalas. Most of the shipping seemed to come from China. Tracking purchases would be virtually impossible. "But I don't think it will get us anywhere."

Just when she thought she had a lead, it seemed an impossible one.

Earle sat next to her, picked up a mug of coffee, and took a sip. He pulled a face. "Sugar."

"Yes, that's mine." She took it from him. "There's something else…" She frowned, remembering the last session with her therapist, Meredith.

"What?"

"Now that you've said about the mandala, and it being Buddhist, Hindu and all that, I saw something…a statue."

"What of?"

"A Buddha. To tell the truth, I haven't thought much more about it, they're everywhere. A popular ornament for anyone, it seems."

He was quiet, nibbling on his bottom lip and with a slight crease between his eyes.

"I mean, just since then," she went on, "I've seen them in Frasers, a restaurant, heck, Fletcher has a little one on his windowsill."

"Does he?"

"Huh, some detective." She poked him on the shoulder and grinned.

He laughed. "Hey, I'm still learning."

She rolled her eyes. Earle was damn good at his job, and he knew it.

"We're doing well here, folks, you need to give me a harder case." Andy held up a notepad as he walked towards them.

"What have you got?" Shona asked.

"This guy talking to Samri Laghari, on CCTV, is Aran Barker, thirty-six years old, born in Middleton."

"Aran Barker," Shona repeated. "Great work. Do we have a present address?"

"Yep, right here in Ironash."

She nodded. The urge to jump up, race to his house, and arrest him was almost overwhelming, but of course, she couldn't do that. Apart from a vision of him whilst she'd been in therapy, she had nothing to arrest him for.

"He's an electrician," Andy went on, "self-employed, does odd jobs. Drives a red Volkswagen Caddy, you know, one of those little van things, four years old."

"Yep." Earle nodded.

"He's got a Tesco Mobile account. I ran a check on his recent calls, nothing of note, but they're here for you anyway." He tapped the notepad with a pen.

"Social media?" Shona asked.

"Nothing, like his mate Samri Laghari, he's invisible. Seems he likes to keep his private life private."

"For good reason." Shona shook her head. "That's great, thanks." She paused. "Are you doing okay? Need to get back to the family?"

"Yeah, I'd better show my face soon." He straightened his black tie. "I found this out, too, on the other name you just gave me, Vince Thomas."

Shona and Earle were silent.

"He's living back in Ironash, with Samir Laghari."

"He is?" Shona's eyes widened.

So they've hooked up again.

"Yes, it said in his rap sheet that he's asthmatic, so I checked in with the local GP. He's registered there and he's put down Samir's address on the form."

"Might not be living there, just using it for treatment," Shona said, hoping that wasn't the case.

"But he might be." Earle stood. "Even if it's just temporary."

"For a few weeks in the summer." Her shoulders were tense, and a dull throb was setting up home in her right temple. She ignored both.

"You need me to do anything else?" Andy asked.

"No, you get off." Shona smiled. "And thanks, I really appreciate your help today."

"I'm around all weekend. You need anything, let me know. I'll come in."

"You sure?" Shona was surprised. Junior officers didn't usually volunteer to give up their weekend.

"Excellent distraction from life," he said. "And it makes me feel good to catch the bad guys."

"You and me both." She dared to allow a sliver of hope to wend its way through her. She had three names, two addresses, and one piece of evidence. Now all she needed was a reason to arrest the bastards, and she had a feeling they were about to give her one.

All she had to do, as Andy had just said, was catch them.

Chapter Seven

"Come on, Duke, we're heading out." Manfred secured Duke's working dog jacket, which he'd been told was neon yellow, and attached the harness. "We have a special ingredient to buy for tonight's dinner, and I want it as fresh as possible."

Duke wagged his tail, and it banged off the hallway radiator, almost knocking over Manfred's white stick. He caught it as it bounced off his thigh, surprising himself that he had.

"Alexa, music off," Manfred called to the kitchen.

Bohemian Rhapsody came to an abrupt halt.

He patted his jeans pocket to make sure his wallet and phone were there, then clicked his tongue, a sign for Duke to move forward.

He pulled the door shut, locked it, then pocketed the keys. The air was fresh after the storm and held a hint of pollen.

"Oh, Mr Napier, good morning."

"Morning, Mrs Hill, how are you?" He tapped his stick, checking he was in the centre of his garden path.

"I'm perfectly well, but I saw the ambulance last night, parked up here. What on earth happened?"

Her voice was high-pitched and screechy. It always grated on Manfred, but today he squashed that irritation down. He needed to act like the distressed ex-colleague, the distraught friend. "It wasn't for me, it was—"

"Thank goodness. You're our dear neighbour and friend, Mr Napier."

If I was your friend, you'd call me Manfred.

"Thank you, Mrs Hill. I had someone I used to work with visiting, for dinner. He became unwell."

"Oh...what was it?"

"His heart, dodgy ticker. We were just sitting enjoy a Scotch, chatting about the good old days, and next thing he keeled over."

"Oh my God, what did you do?"

"Well, obviously I wasn't the greatest person to have to hand." He gestured to his melted eyes, now hidden behind dark glasses. "But I called an ambulance."

"With your Alexa thingy?"

He paused. Could he have done that? He had no idea.

"No, I just used Siri on my phone." He dragged in a deep breath, allowed it to judder out, hoping that showed the memory was painful. "But unfortunately it was too late."

She sucked in air. "Oh dear Lord, really? He died...here, on our very street?"

"I'm afraid so."

"That's terrible. Does he have a family?"

"Yes, a wife, Gloria. I'm just going to get her some flowers." He probably should, it would make him appear more sympathetic to the situation. "Poor thing, she'll be devastated."

Actually, she would be. They didn't have children. She really was all alone now.

For a moment Manfred felt a bit bad about that. He hadn't considered Gloria when he'd plotted to kill her husband. She'd always been smiley and friendly when he'd bumped into her. Well...when he could see, that was. He hadn't been in her company since the day the Fucking Useless Four had shown the depths of their uselessness.

"It just goes to show, we're all at God's mercy. We go but for the grace of Him. Never know when your number might be up." Mrs Hill tutted. "Given me the shivers to tell you the truth. Not nice to have death on the street, is it?"

"No, it really isn't."

You'd better get used to it.

He nodded a goodbye then stepped out onto the pavement. He turned left towards Blighty Bingo. Beyond that was a Greggs. Once he'd been to Waitrose, he'd treat himself to a warm chicken-and-bacon slice. He'd get a sausage roll for Duke, too—shouldn't really, but the poor mite had hated the storm, he deserved a treat.

Progress was slow, what with the stick and Duke stopping to sniff several lampposts—he shouldn't, but Manfred was soft on him—but eventually he arrived at the supermarket.

He picked up a basket with a rising sense of anticipation. He had another meal to cook tonight. This time it was for moaning Fredrick. What would the main complaint be? His latest holiday to Spain, the hot weather, the rising price of fuel? Perhaps he'd have some new material, witter on about the fact England were losing in the Euros or the Prime Minister was a prick.

Which Manfred wouldn't disagree with.

He found his way to the meat counter and asked for two rump steaks.

Another last supper so only the best.

After that, he tracked down a shop assistant and had her add carrots, new potatoes, a raspberry jelly, and a pack of strawberries.

"Are they nice and red, no bad ones?" he asked.

"Yes, sir, they're all perfect, the best punnet here."

"Thank you, they're for a friend who has a particular thing for strawberries. I'm making him tea."

"Ah, that's nice. You're very kind."

"Thank you."

"I hope you have a lovely tea party. The sun is out—maybe you could have it in the garden, *Alice in Wonderland* style."

Manfred smiled. It was weird how some people treated him childlike. If only they could see into his black heart, hear his dark, murderous thoughts. Not so childish after all, eh!

After a visit to Greggs, Manfred tapped his way home. The shopping had taken longer than he'd thought, and once in his kitchen, he ate his slice hungrily and washed it down with two mugs of tea.

Duke scoffed his sausage roll in seconds then spent ages snuffling around for crumbs.

"Alexa, what are the signs of anaphylactic shock?"

"According to the NHS website, anaphylaxes usually develops suddenly and gets worse very quickly. Symptoms include light-headedness, feeling faint, shortness of breath, wheezing, tightness of chest, rapid heartbeat, anxiety, and losing consciousness. There may be other symptoms, including itching raised rash, feeling or being sick, stomach pain."

Manfred finished his tea and stood. He flicked on the kettle and tipped the contents of the jelly packet into a jug. He then found a sieve and began to wash the strawberries.

"Alexa, play *Strawberry Fields Forever*."

"*Strawberry Fields Forever* by the Beatles from Spotify."

Manfred hummed to the tune as he washed, dried, then added four of the strawberries to the mortar. After mashing them with the pestle and enjoying their sweet scent, he added them to the jelly mixture, poured in the boiling water, and gave it a good stir. He left the jelly packet out, so Fredrick could be assured of the ingredients later.

"Fredrick, hello, how nice of you to come."

"Well, I nearly didn't, Mannie." Fredrick stepped into the house, the scent of Marlborough Lights swirling in with him. "Beryl called. Told me about Terry. I can't believe it's true." He sniffed, as though he was genuinely upset. "I mean...really...he's dead?"

"Afraid so."

"And it was here?" There was a gravelly quality to his voice, one Manfred hadn't noticed before.

Is he really that upset about stupid Terry?

Duke pushed between them, sniffing Fredrick.

"Yes, to tell you the truth," Manfred said, slipping back into character. "I'm quite shook up, so I am glad you came. For the company and all that. I keep going over and over it in my mind. It's like that when you live alone, you ruminate on stuff."

After a few seconds a ring pull hissed open, then another. Fredrick pressed a cold can into Manfred's hands.

"Thanks." He took a slurp then caught a dribble that escaped from the right side of his wonky mouth.

"I should take some flowers to Gloria," Fredrick said, "see if she needs a hand with the funeral."

A chair scraped on the kitchen floor. Manfred imagined Fredrick sitting, crossing his long spindly legs then chugging on his beer.

"Yes, I thought the same." He set the pan on the now hot ring. "Not that I'm much use to anyone."

"Don't say that, Mannie."

A silence fell.

"Let's have some music," Manfred said. "Alexa, play *Knocking on Heaven's Door*."

"Playing *Knocking on Heaven's Door* from Spotify."

The strum of a guitar filled the kitchen.

"This was one of Terry's favourites," Manfred said.

"Was it? I didn't know."

Manfred smiled and dropped the steaks into the pan. The potatoes and carrots were pre-done. All he had to do was heat them.

"You think you know everything about someone," Fredrick said. "And that they'll always be there."

"How do you like yours done?"

"Er, medium, please."

"Okay, it won't be long."

"When do you think the funeral will be?" Fredrick asked.

"Next week, I expect. There's nothing untoward, no suspicious circumstances, so it will be a speedy process."

Fredrick sighed. "Poor sod. He had so much life left in him."

"Clearly not. He must have had a bad heart, a problem he didn't know about."

"He seemed okay."

"Well, yes...of course. Beryl's coming round tomorrow, she said."

Yep. So I can do her in, too.

"The last thing we want," Fredrick went on, "is for you to suffer more than you already have, Mannie."

"Thank you." He shut the door. "But what's done is done. All we can hope is that our streak of bad luck has come to an end." He led the way to the kitchen, sliding his hand along the dado rail in the hallway. "I mean, that's two of us..."

"At least you're alive."

If you count being a monster alive.

"True, and I can't help wondering if I should have done more. I mean...if I wasn't blind, would I have seen the signs?"

"You mustn't think like that, Mannie."

"It's impossible not to ponder, wonder about the what-ifs."

Fredrick squeezed his shoulder as they went into the kitchen. "My old ma told me a long time ago, no point in what-ifs."

Manfred puffed out a long, low sigh, emptying his lungs. "I've got us a rump steak each. Is that okay?"

"Yeah, good for me. Some people can't eat when they're upset. I'm the opposite. First thing I did when I heard the news was reach for a pizza."

"I'm the same."

What a freak.

"I'll start cooking, shall I?"

"Go for it. I brought a four-pack. Just out the fridge. Want one?"

"Please." Manfred tapped around the table, found the jelly packet. "I've made us raspberry jelly for dessert, to go with salted caramel ice cream. Comfort food and all that."

"Boy, I'm bloody glad you got raspberry. You know me and strawberries, a match made in Hell."

Manfred smiled. "Check the ingredients."

"Isn't that often the way?" He scooped the dinners onto two plates. "Here you go. I've timed it, three minutes each side, usually makes it medium."

"I'll have a look." Pause. Scrape of a knife. "Perfect, thank you. Shall we toast our old mate, Terry?"

"Definitely." Manfred located his can and held it up.

Fredrick knocked his against it. "To Terry."

"To Terry."

They began to eat. The song ended.

"Alexa, play *Candle in the Wind*."

"*Candle in the Wind* by Elton John from Spotify."

Piano music echoed around the kitchen.

"Oh, for fuck's sake," Fredrick groaned. "This'll have me bawling."

"Terry liked it, though. Funny that I remember his favourites and you don't. He had that picture of Marilyn Monroe on his locker, that one with her in the white dress, blowing up and showing her sexy legs."

"Ah, yes, you're right. Had good taste did our Terry."

They carried on eating, Elton's dulcet tones accompanying them.

When he'd finished, Manfred set his knife and fork down. His stomach was satisfyingly full, and the meat gave his mouth a glossy, silky feel.

Duke was sitting at his feet, clearly hoping for scraps. Bloody dog ate anything and everything, except for sprouts. He could pick them out of the scraps of a meal and spit them to one side.

"That was delicious," Fredrick said. "Cheers for that. I know they're not cheap, the Waitrose steaks."

"We deserved a treat."

"Too right. Here, let me clear these. Can I give Duke the last bits?"

"Yes, he'll love you forever if you do that."

"I'll take love wherever I can get it."

Manfred opened the fridge and retrieved the now set jelly. He found the ice cream and filled two bowls with each.

Duke was wolfing down the remnants of their dinner.

"Jelly and ice cream takes me back to being a kid," Fredrick said at Manfred's side.

"Take one, I think they're about the same."

"Yeah, perfect."

Manfred stared straight ahead. Like last night, the anticipation became a real living force within him. His heart clattered along. His skin tingled. And his breaths were coming quick, as if he'd just run up the stairs.

This shouldn't take long.

"Salted caramel is the best. What did we do before it?" Fredrick said. The spoon clanked off his teeth.

"I agree." Manfred slid some jelly into his mouth. He let it roll around the inside of his cheeks and over his tongue. It wasn't quite the masterpiece the hollandaise sauce had been—he hadn't taken into account the strawberry pips, he could feel them.

"Wow, strong flavour jelly," Fredrick said.

"You like it?"

"Mmm…" He cleared his throat. "I do."

"We'll have a Sotch after. You're not driving, are you?"

"No, I'm not driving."

Manfred sensed him standing. "Everything okay?"

"No."

A bang. As if he'd lurched into the kitchen counter.

Duke barked.

"Fredrick. What is it?"

"The jelly…I think…it must have strawberry…in it."

"Shit." He paused. "What can I do?"

"I didn't bring my…EpiPen…fuck…"

Duke barked again and bumped into Manfred.

"But I asked the shop assistant to get me raspberry."

"I know, and it is, but it must have..." Fredrick made a strange wheezing sound, as though the air couldn't get through the channel of his throat.

I know what that feels like you bastard.

"I can't..."

"Bloody hell. What shall I do?" Manfred asked.

"I need...am...am...ambulance."

Another clatter and then a smash. He was staggering around, bashing into stuff.

Manfred wondered about trying out Alexa to ring an ambulance, but it was too soon. He needed the second of the Fucking Useless Four to be dead before he summoned the emergency services.

Fredrick was gurgling and falling around the kitchen. He lurched into Manfred who staggered and sent his bowl of ice cream and jelly flying. It clattered to the floor. Duke scooted past him.

And then a solid thump told Manfred his victim was down.

Quickly, he dropped to his knees, felt around, found Fredrick.

His breaths were tight gasps, as if he had an elastic band around his neck.

"It's okay, I'll call the ambulance," Manfred said.

"Too...late..."

Yes, it was. Manfred didn't need to be able to see to know Fredrick was taking his last breaths. And as he lay there, dying, he'd understand what it had been like for Manfred to be sprawled on the floor of Colour Me Happy with his face and eyeballs melting and pain beyond comprehension stabbing at his entire body.

Oh yes, now he'd know. Now he'd understand that incompetence, not checking things properly, could result in disaster...could result in death.

"Alexa, play *Don't Fear The Reaper*."

"Playing *Don't Fear The Reaper* by Blue Öyster Cult from Spotify."

Haunting guitar music and soul-filled lyrics filled the kitchen, accompanying Fredrick's last gasping attempts to breathe.

"Death is inevitable," Manfred said, resting his hand on Fredrick's chest. "We all know that."

Duke nudged him, his fur soft on Manfred's arm. "Hey, mate, I hope you're going to eat up all the jelly and ice cream like a good boy. Don't want evidence lying about, do we." He laughed, a loud release of tension.

Fredrick's chest stilled. The gurgling sounds coming from his throat ceased.

Manfred was halfway there. Only two more to go. And if all went to plan, each death would be considered an accident. Stranger things happened, right. And him, a poor old blind man, what harm could he do anyone?

Chapter Eight

"We should swing by," Shona said into the phone as she munched a muesli bar the next morning, "take a look at Samri's house from the outside, see if there's anything going on. Aran Barker's, too."

"It's Saturday," Earle replied.

"I haven't got anything on, and this case, it's time-sensitive." She thought of the phone call from Ben—him asking her to help out at the dojo and then go for lunch. Probably she should. All work and no play made Shona a dull girl. But she was twitchy with the case, *her* case. And she had a limited window of opportunity. History showed there could be another attack soon, very soon. "But if you have cakes to bake or need to take a trip to Manchester, then that's okay, I'll go on my—"

"Nope, nothing going on, and yeah, you're right, we should check those addresses out."

"Unless you—"

"I'm free, all good." There was determination in his tone. "I'll pick you up in half an hour."

"Perfect."

She ended the call and hit dial on Ben's number.

He answered after two rings.

"Hi, Ben, it's Shona."

"Good morning, how are you?" He was bright and cheerful.

"I'm fine thanks, but I'm not going to make it today."

He was quiet.

"Something's come up, with work, you know how it is. Bad guys don't run to a nine-to-five, Monday-to-Friday schedule."

"No, course they don't. That's okay." He paused. "A drink tonight maybe, in town?"

She stared out of the conservatory window at her mother's neat lawn complete with stripes. "Maybe, but..." Truth was, she didn't want to commit, and a drink out on a Saturday night sounded scarily like a date.

"But what?" he asked.

"This work thing...might go on a bit. Can we do it another time?"

"Of course. You take care now, see you at the next senior training session."

"Yes, have a nice day."

He hung up.

She sighed. She wasn't playing hard to get deliberately. She had to focus on catching the bastards who'd ruined her and her two best friends' lives. And dating...she was hardly in the habit of going out with men. Not that she didn't have plenty of offers, but turning them down had become a habit she was comfortable with.

But something about Ben was different. He tugged her into the 'say yes' direction, and she wasn't used to that. Perhaps when she'd solved this case—and she *would* solve it—she'd be able to loosen up and have what other women her age had—a boyfriend.

Thirty minutes later, she was climbing into Earle's colossal four-by-four.

"Hardly inconspicuous, are we," she said.

"We won't park directly outside." He handed her a cupcake topped with swirling lemon-yellow icing.

"Oh, nice, what's this for?"

"You seem to be craving sugar at the moment."

"Yes, must be the adrenaline. I feel like I'm getting closer...the closest I've ever been. It's making me twitchy."

"You still okay to hang on with Vince Thomas?"

"You mean not arrest him despite having that DNA evidence?"

"Yeah."

She scooped a chunk of icing onto her finger and sucked it off. "Yes, for now. I'm hoping he'll lead us into a situation where we can pin something on all three of them."

"I like your thinking."

He pulled away, and after edging through the busy Saturday shopper's traffic, they came to Scooners, the sprawling estate on the opposite side of Ironash. It wasn't as pretty as where Shona's parents lived, no trees lining the avenues. The parade of shops had metal shutters which were dropped down at night. It wasn't unusual to see a car on bricks in a front garden, or a window with a board over it.

They turned down a cul-de-sac bursting with parked vehicles.

"Bugger," Earle said.

"It's okay, slip into that gap at the end, by that row of garages. If someone asks us to move, we'll flash them our ID."

"Okay."

He parked up, and Shona was glad of his darkened windows as they surveyed the street.

A group of kids were playing on bikes and scooters. They'd set up a ramp with a breeze block and a length of sheet metal. A skinny brown dog wandered around on its own, and a black bin bag of rubbish had spilled onto the pavement. A magpie was pulling at the contents.

"Number eighteen, right?" Shona said.

"Yep, the one in the corner."

She'd already figured that out and was studying it. The door was red; the one window downstairs had the curtains closed. Upstairs were two windows. One had a blind drawn down, the other didn't appear to have any kind of curtain, and books were stacked on the sill. "That's his van there, right?"

Earle flicked open his notebook. "It's his registration."

"Maybe he had a late night, still asleep." She twisted the empty wrapper of her cupcake.

"Could be a long wait."

They sat in silence, studying the house, watching the kids, the dog, and the magpie.

After an hour, the upstairs blind was drawn up. An outline flashed behind the glass, but Shona couldn't be sure it was Samri.

She suppressed a shudder.

"How long are we going to wait?" Earle asked.

"Until you need to go and get on with your weekend."

"I'm okay." He folded his arms.

She bit on her bottom lip, glanced at him. "Did you hear back from Patrick?"

"No."

"He probably hasn't got his phone with him, or it's in a locker or something."

"Probably."

It was clear Earle didn't want to talk, so she returned her focus to number eighteen.

After a few minutes with just the children's distant voices to listen to, Earle spoke again. "Look who's coming?"

"Bloody hell. It's Vince Thomas."

Sure enough, sauntering down the street was the bloke she had a mugshot of. His jeans were ripped at the knees, and his black t-shirt had an image of a big red hand giving the finger. His baseball cap was on back to front, and dark hair stuck out messily over his ears and at his nape.

"Seems he is around after all." Earle rubbed his hands.

"Good, I want them all together and then I want to pin them down."

"Metaphorically or with a karate chop?"

"Both actually." She huffed.

Vince wandered up to Samri's house and let himself in. A minute later, the curtains were opened in the living room.

Is that where I was taken? Is there a Buddha and a mandala in that room? Does it smell of spices?

She balled her hands into fists. There was no way of knowing for definite, but it was a good bet that she'd been in there before and not because she'd wanted to be.

Her phone vibrated in her pocket. She pulled it out. "Hey, Darren, what's up."

"Apart from the fact it's my birthday weekend and I'm at work covering sickness?"

"Ah, sorry about that."

"Not your fault."

She was quiet.

"Got a funny one, thought you'd want to know."

"Go on."

"Might be something, might be nothing. An address on Drover Road has had two ambulance call-outs, each resulting in a death."

"Causes?"

"One a suspected heart attack and the other an allergic reaction."

"Sounds legit." She watched for movement in the downstairs window.

"The call-outs were a night apart. It's a single guy who lives alone, Manfred Napier, sixty-six." He paused. "Just seemed a bit odd to me, or damn unlucky, so thought I'd throw it out there."

"Yes, you're right, a night apart is odd." She glanced at Earle. "Text me the address and details. We'll pop round; we're in work mode so it's no problem."

"Aren't we all."

She ended the call.

"What's going on?" Earle asked.

"Two fatalities at the same address, medical by the sound of it, but only a night apart."

"Mmm, that is a bit strange."

Her phone bleeped. She flashed the address at Earle. "Know where this is?"

"Yeah." He started the engine. "I take it we're going to say hello."

Manfred Napier's bungalow was set in a neat row of similar houses and lined with a squat brick wall. The front garden had been gravelled, low maintenance, and there was no car on the drive.

Beside the doorbell was a sign: Beware of the Dog.

"Hope it's not a staffy," Earle said, pressing the bell. "Can't bear those."

"No?"

"Nope, went to a call-out once. Let's just say kids and staffy's don't mix."

"Urgh, horrible. And just why…I mean, why risk it?"

But there was no dog's bark.

Earle pressed the doorbell again.

This time there was one deep woof, and after a few seconds the door opened.

Standing before them, in the dim light of the hallway, was a tall man wearing black-lensed glasses. His face was distorted. The shiny pink skin raised in some places, dipped in others, and his lips were askew.

"Manfred Napier?" Shona averted her gaze so he wouldn't think she was staring.

"Yes. Who are you?" His voice was gruff, as though speaking over sandpaper.

She flipped open her ID and held it forward.

He continued to stare straight ahead. A golden retriever appeared at his side, intelligent bright eyes, pink tongue hanging out.

Earle glanced at her and raised his eyebrows.

"I'm sorry, you are…?" Manfred said, resting his hand on the dog's head.

"We're the police," Shona said, still holding forward the ID. "I'm DI Shona Williams, this is DS Earle Montague."

"Oh, there's two of you."

"Yes, sir." She understood the dark glasses now, and the dog at his side. "Would it be possible to come in?"

"Why?"

"A few routine questions. Nothing to worry about."

"I haven't done anything wrong."

"No one is saying any such thing, but there have been two ambulance call-outs to this address, each resulting in a fatality. It's routine for us to check on you, ensure you're okay after the incidents."

"Ah, that is very kind. Of course, come in." He stepped backwards. "Duke, come on now, let these nice people inside."

They followed him down a narrow hall, past several closed doors and into a kitchen. It had a nice big window looking over the secluded back garden. This was lawned and had a shed and a hot tub—one of the expensive big solid ones. A glossy holly bush stood in one corner and buddleia dotted with butterflies in another. The fences were high and appeared freshly painted.

Music was playing, an intense piano piece, classical. She wasn't sure what it was from but reckoned it would suit a horror movie.

"Alexa, music off."

The kitchen fell silent.

"Great things, these voice-activated assistants." Shona nodded at the small round gadget.

"Couldn't be without it." Manfred reached for the kettle. "I've got it connected to the house—smart house, they call it. Well, it is kind of, does the lights and heating for me."

"Useful." Shona folded her arms and glanced around.

The kitchen work surfaces were clean and uncluttered. A small table with two chairs was pushed up against the wall. A large chrome fridge held a single magnet shaped like a dart. There appeared to be a splash of pink goo on the wall, a long drip shape.

"Have you always been blind?" she asked.

"No." He filled the kettle. "I take it you want tea?"

"Please, that would be lovely." Shona stooped and picked up a red packet. Raspberry jelly. She placed it on the worktop.

"I had an accident, nearly two years ago now," Manfred said. "At work."

"I'm sorry." Duke was sniffing her feet with enthusiasm. She hated it when dogs did that. "What happened?"

"An aerosol paint can, hadn't been assembled properly. There's a lot of pressure in those things, a lot of flammable ingredients, too." He touched his lips, the right side, which were enlarged and sloped downwards. "Damn thing exploded when I was checking it for quality control." He paused.

Earle and Shona shared a look.

"It took out my eyes, and as you can see left me with this not-so-pretty face. Galling thing about the whole incident was I had retirement in my sights. It was only a stone's throw away."

"I'm so sorry," Shona said, stepping away from Duke and letting him move onto Earle's shoes. "Did you get compensation?"

"Yes, a decent payout. Sorted out the last of my mortgage, got divorced years ago, and had to start again after giving her a chunk of my cash. Treated myself to a few things to make life more bearable." He pointed outside. "Hot tub, electric lawn mower, new fences so the neighbours don't have to put up with my ugly mug. Not that money is as much fun when you can't see. Never have seen the point of holidays since the accident, and at one time I would have blown a fair bit on a fancy car—again, not much point."

"Was the accident anyone's fault?" she asked.

"No, it was a catalogue of errors, you know, tiny things that added up."

The kettle came to the boil.

"Tea all round?" he asked.

"Yes, would you like me to make it?"

"No, no, I'm perfectly capable in the kitchen, just takes me a bit of time. But I love to cook." He paused. "I love to cook for my friends. It's one of the few pleasures I have left."

Earle produced his notebook and pen.

"And it was friends who were visiting, who required the ambulance?"

"Yes." He sighed and pressed his hand to his chest. "Dear friends, old colleagues. I'm devastated, as you can imagine."

"I'm sorry for your loss. Can you tell me what happened with Mr...?"

"Terry Smith." Earle read from his pad.

"Poor Terry." Manfred turned away. "We just never knew that he had a problem with his heart." His shoulders juddered, as if emotion was being released from them. "All that time...wandering around with a defect..."

"Can you tell me what happened?" Shona asked. This poor guy was clearly upset.

"I can tell you what I heard." He reached into the fridge and produced a small carton of milk.

She waited for him to go on.

"We'd finished our salmon, had a good old chat about times gone by—Terry always could talk for Britain. And then he said he felt unwell, hot, like, and that his chest hurt. Naturally I was concerned, asked what I could do. He said nothing...after that it all happened so quickly. He went into the living room, and I heard him crash to the floor. By the time I got there he was out of it. I called an ambulance, loosened his clothing like they do on TV, and..."

"And?"

"It was too late. By the time the paramedics got here, I knew he was gone. Ohhhh, his poor family. It's just awful, really it is. And Gloria is such a sweetheart. I feel terrible, responsible almost."

"It's not your fault, Mr Napier. Sadly these things happen." She took the tea. "Thank you."

"DS Montague." Manfred held another cup forward.

"Thanks." Earle took it. "Can you tell us about Fredrick Deans?"

"Certainly." He faced the worktop again and picked up his tea. He seemed to stare outside for a moment, shoulders shaking a little as he cradled the mug. "The tragic thing is, he came around because he'd heard about Terry, didn't want me on my own. Such a nice guy, the best. I can't believe he's gone, too." He sniffed then sipped his drink.

"What did you do together, while he was here?" Shona asked.

"We were sad, obviously, probably still in shock. I cooked, tried to do something normal, take my mind off it. I did us a steak each, nice bit of rump from Waitrose, figured we needed cheering up."

Duke flopped into a soft brown bed beside the radiator.

"It was good to talk about our friend, and I was glad of the company. But then…oh God, it was awful, like history repeating itself. I made us jelly and ice cream, comfort food, you know, and it's so hot this week. It was raspberry jelly, because Fredrick is…was…allergic to strawberries. I left the packet out, so he could check it, make sure it was something he could eat but… I just don't know how to explain it? I mean, can someone just develop another allergy?"

"I guess the coroner will have the answers to that question." Shona picked up the jelly packet and studied the ingredients. No strawberry.

"It was just like with Terry. It happened so fast. One minute he was chatting away, the next he was struggling to breathe. Again I called an ambulance…again I was too late." He sat at the table, removed his glasses, and pressed his hands over his face. He appeared defeated, desperate, and still in shock.

"We really are very sorry you had to go through this," Shona said, setting the weak tea to one side. She didn't really fancy it.

"How could it happen?" He shook his head. "Two of my best friends gone. I'm going to miss them so much. They were so good to me, so good...the best."

"I can put you in touch with a grief counsellor," Shona said. "If you'd like that."

"I think I would." He replaced his glasses. "I'm already lonely and now...now I'm struggling to know how to carry on."

"Do you have anyone else? Any family?"

"No, I live alone. My wife and I didn't have children, she didn't want them." He sighed. "I do have a couple of other friends, from my work days, but they're busy with life."

"Perhaps you could get in touch with them. It's helpful to talk."

"Yes, you're right."

Earle stepped up to the sink and tipped his tea away. He pulled a face at Shona.

"We'll be off then, Mr Napier. As long as you're okay."

"I will be...thank you."

"I'll get that counsellor to give you a call or pop round."

"When will that be?"

"Probably not until next week now."

"Ah, okay."

"Will you be all right until then?"

"Yes... I'll manage." He stood.

"Please, stay there, we'll show ourselves out."

"Okay, Officer."

Duke got to his feet, then followed them down the hallway. He waited patiently by the door as they opened it then went out into the heat of the day.

"Poor bugger," Earle said as they walked to the car. "That's one hell of a workplace injury."

"Yes, really nasty." Shona touched her own lips. "Though I guess he can't see how disfigured he is."

"Silver lining." Earle climbed into the car.

Shona did the same. She looked out of the window at the small neat house with its straight little garden path. "Two deaths in two days, that's really bad luck, eh?"

"I agree." Earle paused. "Do you think he had anything to do with it? Should we be suspicious?"

"Nah, he's harmless. Must be hard enough to get through everyday life when you can't see. Chances of him being able to get up to no good are slim to none."

"True."

"Come on, let's go and get a decent cup of tea. That was just hot water with milk. After that, we'll go and have a nose at where Aran Barker lives."

Chapter Nine

Manfred listened to the two police officers drive away. Sounded like a big gutsy car, a four-by-four, off-roader perhaps. He'd guess it belonged to the bloke. She'd sounded small and sweet. He got the feeling her partner was tall and not lacking in the muscle department.

Their turning up hadn't been a complete surprise. Terry and Fredrick passing away on his property was always going to raise flags, but luckily, he'd covered his tracks. There was no way he could be under suspicion. A scarred old blind man just wanting a bit of company. Not exactly *Psycho* was it?

"Well done, Duke, you go out the back for a wee now." He opened the door.

Someone was mowing their lawn in the distance. The heater for the hot tub had come on as it did each day—it was on a timer so it was always warm in the evening should he want to use it. The low hum didn't bother him if he sat in the garden, he could always turn it off. The little robotic mower was more of a nuisance.

He felt over the surface of the worktop and came across the jelly packet. He'd left it on the floor—seemed one of the detectives had picked it up. Excellent. He'd bet good money they'd checked the ingredients.

Shame they hadn't checked the back of the fridge.

He opened the door, chuckled, and reached for the strawberries. He tipped them into a bowl, then sprinkled sugar on the top.

Best get rid of the evidence.

Once he'd eaten, he located his phone and used Siri to call Beryl.

"Oh, Mannie, how are you?" she said after only one ring. "I just heard about Fredrick, and with Terry, too..."

"It's terrible, really it is." Manfred paused and forced what he hoped sounded like a sob out of his throat. "I'm distraught."

"Of course you are, you poor dear."

Poor dear!

"It's a terrible thing to happen," she went on, "two tragic accidents in two days. I mean...what will become of Colour Me Happy?"

"They're certainly going to be down in staffing numbers." The truth was, Manfred couldn't care less what happened to the stupid company or the stupid owners. It had taken him ages to get his compensation. They'd kicked up a stink about him not wearing his damn safety goggles. How would they like to wear those things all day every day?

"I just wanted to say," he said, "I totally understand if you don't want to come for dinner tonight, Beryl. It's a lot to take in...so, so sad."

"It really is horribly sad, but I'm worried about you, Mannie. I don't want you to get that...what's it called...STD or something."

"PTSD, and yes, I do feel quite traumatised."

"Of course you do, and I'll be there later. Friends need to stick together at times like this."

"Are you sure?"

"Yes, of course. Can't guarantee how much I'll eat, my appetite's gone a bit, but I'll come round. About eight okay?"

"Yes, perfect. And thank you. I really appreciate it."

"It will do us both good. We were close to Terry and Fredrick. I can't believe they're gone."

"Me neither." He paused. "Hot tub's warm. If you don't want to eat you can use that."

"I might." She sighed. "It's always so soothing."

"I agree. See you later."

At seven-thirty, Manfred fed Duke, ensured the Pinot had chilled sufficiently, and checked the PH of the hot tub. His small bleeper told him it was perfect. Beryl always liked the hot tub, said it made her night out a mini holiday.

She was so damn weird.

He'd put a casserole in the oven, only Cumberland sausages with some diced potato and carrots. Not really a mid-summer meal, but if he was hungry later, it would do.

Duke barked when the doorbell rang then rushed into the hallway, his paws tapping on the wooden flooring.

Manfred followed him, pausing to put his dark glasses on before opening the door.

"Oh, Mannie." Beryl threw herself at him. "This is so tragic."

Her skinny body pressed against his, and her stick-like arms coiled around his waist. It took all of his willpower not to shove her away.

Gross.

"It really is." He stroked her bony shoulder, his muscles going rigid and his jaw tensing.

"Honestly, I cried all the way here, and it's a thirty-minute walk. I'm actually quite glad you can't see me."

You're glad I can't see? Thanks for that, bitch.

"You need to debrief." She drew back from him. "And I've brought us a bottle of white to do that with."

"Excellent, I have some as well, so we won't run dry."

He stepped to one side so she could enter the house. "Did Brian mind you coming out tonight?"

"No, he's gone to the dogs with the Nelson brothers, you know what they're like on a Saturday night."

"Yeah, they like a flutter, don't they." He shut the door.

"I don't approve, but as long as he stays sensible." She paused. "Hi, Duke, how are you doing?"

Duke was winding around them, his tail wafting the air.

"I think he's a bit upset, too," Manfred said, "all that fuss, the ambulance, me being frantic and all that."

"They say animals pick up on that sort of stuff. I saw it on a programme once."

"I'm sure they do, and guide dogs are especially sensitive to human emotion, they're trained that way."

"Ah, bless him."

They walked into the kitchen, Beryl leading the way.

"Shall I pour?" she said.

"Go ahead, you know where the glasses are."

As she opened the wine, Manfred tipped a jumbo packet of Twiglets into a serving dish. "I haven't spoken to Gloria but I sent her flowers."

"Poor thing is going to be lost without her Terry. They were planning a cruise for their anniversary, you know."

"No, I didn't know. Where were they going?"

"Caribbean, a trip of a lifetime."

Should have done it while he was alive.

"So sad." He shook his head. "Tragic, in fact."

"I expect the funeral will be next week. Want me to pick you and Duke up?"

"Er…" Manfred hadn't thought about going to the funerals, but he supposed he should. He was, in theory, their friend. "Yes, please, that would be kind of you."

"No problem." She sighed as the wine glugged into the glasses. "Are you okay?"

"No, not really, but I doubt I'm feeling as bad as you, Mannie."

"I feel kind of numb, in shock."

And pretty damn pleased with myself.

"Here, get this down you." She pressed a glass into his hand. "To Terry and Fredrick." She clinked her glass on his then swallowed loudly, taking several big gulps.

Manfred took a sip of his. It was sweeter than he liked. "The tub is ready, or do you want to eat?"

"Oh no, I couldn't eat. Sorry, my guts have been giving me hell since I heard the news. Really rumbling, you know, as if there's a big ball of gas rolling around, bumping into all of my organs and trying to get out. Kind of like an explosion waiting to happen."

To much information…again.

"Oh dear, well, have a few Twiglets to go with your wine so you're not drinking on an empty stomach, then we'll get in the tub."

"I'll skip the Twiglets, they give me the burbs. Can I use your bedroom to put my cozzie on?"

"Of course, go and get changed. I'll take the lid off the tub."

He sensed her leave the room and he went into the back garden. The heat had gone from the day, but the birds were still flitting around, and in the distance an ice cream van paraded its tune.

He felt around for the clips on the hot tub then opened the lid. It folded backwards on its big hinge, and despite being heavy was an easy glide into position. The heady scent of chlorine rose upwards, and he breathed deep.

Manfred loved his hot tub, it had been something he'd always wanted. And now, it was one of the few pleasures he didn't need to be able to see to enjoy. When the heat and bubbles surrounded his body it gave him a rare sense of contentment.

"Ah, that is gonna be so good." Beryl was beside him. "You getting in?"

"Yeah, I'll go and put my trunks on."

A few splashes told him she'd climbed straight in.

"Ah, it's so heavenly," she said. "If only…" She sniffed. "If only Terry and Fredrick were still here to enjoy it."

"I know." He rubbed his forehead, as if trying to force away a grief headache. "It's still hard to accept we'll never see them again." He turned and walked slowly, head bowed, spine stooped, feet dragging, to the house.

Once in the kitchen, he allowed the waiting grin to spread and ruffled Duke behind the ears. "Tragedy is always close by."

A few minutes later he was in the hot tub with Beryl and sipping on his too-sweet wine.

Beryl started waffling on about some joke Fredrick had played on Terry the month before. Something about cling film over the toilet. Sounded stupid, and as she spoke, he couldn't quite tell if she was trying not to laugh or cry.

"Have you heard from Darrell?" Manfred asked when she paused to pour more wine.

"He's been on holiday, playing golf in Portugal. So I left him a message. Hated telling him that kind of news on a voicemail, but what choice did I have?"

"I agree, not ideal."

"But he needs to know, otherwise, what will he think when he goes to work on Monday and there's just us two? Me and him holding the fort."

"Oh, Beryl, that's going to be so hard." He hoped he'd injected enough sympathy into his voice. Because in actual fact, he thought that would be pretty bloody funny.

"I know, and I mean, we're hardly the luckiest workforce in the country. What with your appalling accident that's left you blind and horrifically disfigured."

Horrifically disfigured. Thanks again, bitch.

"And now two deaths, heart attack and allergic reaction. It's ghastly, really it is." She burped, loudly. "Ooops, sorry."

"No problem."

"Here, I'll top you up again."

"Thanks."

"It's making me feel a bit better, the wine," she said.

"Good. I'm glad you came, really I am."

"It's no bother." She paused. "Although my Brian wouldn't ordinarily let me spend my Saturday night in a hot tub with another bloke."

"He wouldn't?" Manfred's blood heated, and it wasn't anything to do with the warm water.

"No, he wouldn't."

"Why not?" Damn, why had he asked that? He knew the answer, and it wasn't one he liked.

"Well, you're...Mannie."

"Which means?" He rolled his shoulders; a knot had formed at the base of his neck. A painful little lump.

"You're safe." She paused. "A friend."

"A friend, but still a male friend."

I'm a disfigured monster who no woman could ever be attracted to...go on, say it.

"Yes, well, of course, a male friend...but..." She gulped her wine then burped once more.

He reached out of the tub and set his drink on the small table. "But what?"

"We go back a long way..."

"True."

"Work colleagues for years."

"But now..." He leaned a little closer to where he visualised her to be. "But now I'm ugly, revoltingly ugly. A disgusting monster."

"What? No, I didn't say that, and it's not true."

"I know it is." He ran his fingertips down his indented cheek and over his puffed, stretched lips. "I don't need to be able to see to know I have a mashed-up, melted face."

"It's not so bad."

"Yes it is, and that's what you wanted to say, that's why Brian doesn't mind you spending time with me in a hot tub. It's not because I can't see you in your swimsuit, it's because he knows how hideous I am. You all do. No woman will ever be attracted to me."

"I don't think you're hideous at all."

"I'm a freak, destined to be alone forever. And it's all because of a series of mistakes at Colour Me Happy."

"I'm sure you'll meet someone, if you just get out a bit."

"Getting out isn't easy when you can't see where you're going."

"But...I could help you more, if you want me to."

He reached out, found her scrawny arm, and held it.

"Mannie." She twisted a little, but he kept hold.

His blood had heated further, as if white-hot electricity was searing through his veins and mixing with all that haemoglobin. A kind of fog was descending into his brain, sliding through the blackness.

"They were stupid, careless, avoidable mistakes," he went on, aware that his lips were twisting with each word. "You and Terry, Fredrick and Darrell were all responsible." He gripped her tighter, enjoying the feel of her fragile arm and delicate bone within his hold.

"Mannie, please, you're..."

"Hurting you? Do you think this didn't hurt?" He pointed at his face, splashing water on his chin. "It hurt like seven shades of Hell, I can tell you."

"But the inquiry, it said it was no one's fault. A terrible accident."

"Of course it's someone's fault. I just can't decide whose...which is why..." He moved closer to her small frame.

"Why?" She shoved at him. "Why what? What do you mean?"

"Why you all have to die. All four of you."

"What?"

"All four of you must pay for what happened to me. Fucking useless, that's what you all are."

"No...please. Mannie, what's got into you?"

"Nothing has got into me, at least nothing that hasn't been there since that day."

She tried to peel his fingers from her arm, then bashed his chest. "Get off, you're scaring me. Really scaring me."

"You think I haven't been scared, petrified? Being blind isn't a laugh a fucking minute, you know." His heart was thudding, his rage increasing by the second. "It's bloody terrifying not being able to see."

"I know that, I just..." She burped. "Please let me...go!"

She was getting loud, too loud. He had to act fast. With his free hand, he grasped her hair then dragged her downwards, so her face went under.

"You think I'm a monster, well, let me tell you, you think right."

She thrashed, writhed, and fought. But skinny little Beryl was no match for him.

He held her firm, not caring that she was kicking and punching beneath the surface. He wished Alexa was near enough for him to ask her how long it would take to drown someone. But the kitchen was too far away. He figured a couple of minutes. Quicker when expending energy the way Beryl was.

She gurgled, as if releasing air. Aimed a punch at his groin but missed. More air bubbled up.

Is the skanky cow farting?

Still he kept a strong hold of her. It was kind of fun. Now she'd know how he'd felt, lying frightened and in burning agony on the factory floor that day. His eyes and face melting, his life changing forever.

She bucked, arching and bowing her spine. But her grey permed hair was proving the perfect tool to keep her down. Manfred steeled himself for what he hoped were the final thrashes, the death throes, and stood, pressing his full weight onto her.

She didn't stand a chance.

And then she quieted, her limbs stilled, and the fight in her body seemed to drain away, like a plug had been pulled.

"Die, bitch," he muttered. Damn, he hoped his neighbour four doors down, the one with the dormer window, wasn't witnessing this. He'd be fucked if she was. But with her arthritis, she'd once told him she rarely went upstairs these days.

Beryl was utterly still, but he was loath to let go. He should keep her under for a few more minutes just to be sure.

But then a terrible stench hit his nose. Rank and nausea-inducing. "Ah fuck, you dirty wench."

She'd shit in his beloved hot tub. It had been the last thing she'd done. Filthy, that was what she was.

"Damn it." He gritted his teeth, warred with himself. He was desperate to get out of there but didn't want to let go...not yet.

But he couldn't hold off anymore. The thought of faeces floating around his body—his waist, legs, arms—was too much. He untangled his fingers from her hair and leapt out. A roll of bile swirled up his gullet, and he did his best to ignore it as he dragged the lid over the hot tub.

With shaking hands, he clipped it into place, trapping dead Beryl in the stinking water. Duke was around his feet, sniffing and snuffling.

This hadn't been what he'd planned—a pillow over her face once she was pissed had been on the agenda. Say she'd fallen asleep drunk and must have stopped breathing. But the silly cow had gone and wittered on about how disfigured he was, implied he wasn't a man anymore, unfuckable, unloveable, and that had yanked his murder chain.

And she'd paid the price.

Quickly, he rushed to the outdoor hose and sprayed himself down, not caring about the cold. This really wasn't ideal, not at all. He could sense problems ahead. He'd have to be careful if he wanted to carry out his plan fully and get away with it.

Chapter Ten

Shona and Earle wandered into Ironash Police Station. They'd swung by Aran Barker's home address on the way. All was quiet and his vehicle not in sight.

But they'd find him. Soon.

"Hey, Darren," Shona called.

He looked up from the reception desk. "Hi, anything of note at Mr Napier's?"

"No, poor bugger is blind as a bat and quite shaken."

"Ah, okay, sorry to waste your time."

"You didn't, not at all. It needed a follow-up."

He smiled and returned his attention to a monitor.

They took the stairs and entered the large open-plan office area. Andy was at his desk, head stooped, hand on a mouse.

"What are you doing here on a sunny Saturday afternoon?" Earle asked, a slight frown marring his brow.

"Had to get out of the house. Thought I could find something to do here."

"That bad, eh?" Shona said.

"Two of my aunts have decided to stay over. It's like a scene from *Macbeth*, all cackles, wails, and brewing around the cauldron, or make that teapot."

"Ah, I see."

He sighed. "I know, I know, I'm a grown man, shouldn't be living with my mother, but since Nadine, that's my wife, or rather soon-to-be ex-wife, decided to hitch up with another bloke, I've had no choice. Well, not if I wanted to let the kids be with their mum."

"Sorry to hear that." Shona's heart went out to him. He really wasn't having much luck. Shame, he was a really nice bloke, too. "But we're glad to have you here."

His face brightened a little. "Why? You got something for me?"

"Apart from keeping an eye on CCTV and ANPR for those three guys we identified yesterday, yes, you could do a background check on Manfred Napier for me."

"Really?" Earle asked.

"Got to cover our arses." Shona shrugged. "I'd say with ninety-nine percent surety he's a harmless old man, but if we've done a check, we'll have dotted the I's and crossed the T's."

"Manfred Napier, on it." Andy wrote the name down.

They headed for the kettle. Earle filled it and flicked it on.

"You could shoot off?" Shona said, suddenly feeling guilty for having him at work at the weekend.

"Nah, I'm okay."

"Sure?"

"Yeah, like Andy, I'm better off with something to do, and company."

She thought of Patrick but decided not to bring his name up again. It was clear Earle was worried, and also evident he didn't want to talk about it.

"Cool, I'm going to go over those other date-rape files again."

He nodded. "I'll crack on with some paperwork. Maybe we'll get a sighting of one of our three arseholes."

"It is Saturday, their preferred day of attack."

He muttered something which sounded like 'fuckers' then sat at his desk, his chair creaking under his weight.

Shona made them both tea and set to the files again. As she read over words that had already ingrained themselves in her mind, her stomach tightened. It was as if her instinct, her intuition, had kicked in. She was close, so close. After all this time. And she sensed that something was about to happen. They were preparing to strike. Anticipation laced the warm air and stroked the hairs on her arms.

But why now?
Why this week every year?

And what the heck does the mandala and Buddha have to do with it?

She finished her tea and applied rose-scented handcream. Andy wandered over.

"Manfred Napier." He set a sheet of paper on her desk. "Sixty-six. Born and bred in Ironash. Divorced. Got a big settlement from Colour Me Happy after a workplace injury. Registered blind."

She nodded.

"No previous other than a speeding ticket two years ago, must have been before his accident."

"Yep, I'd imagine so. Can you leave a message for family support to call round. He's had a crap time, might need a chat. We can do without a suicide to deal with."

"On it."

"Perfect, thanks." She set her hand over the sheet of paper with all the information. Mr Napier was a poor old soul who she could push from her mind now. She had other things to think about.

The afternoon stretched into evening, and shadows stretched over the quiet office. When her stomach rumbled, she pressed her palm over it.

"Pizza?" Earle asked.

"Actually, that sounds like a good idea. My parents are out with friends tonight, so I was only looking forward to a bowl of soup."

"Soup, in this weather." Earle laughed. "Come on, let's go and eat something horrifically calorific."

They organised themselves and stopped at Andy's desk on the way to the stairs.

"Hey, you should go home," Shona said. "Or join us for pizza?"

"Not hungry, and I'll head off soon."

Somehow, she didn't believe him. He had three monitors on the go, all showing grainy images of Ironash High Street. He was studying them intently.

"This is the time the bad guys come out to play," he said.

"Duty reception can keep an eye on this."

"Yep, but it's easy to get distracted down there."

"True." She peered at the screens. "Anything of note?"

"A few of the usual troublemakers. I'll stay in touch with uniform about those."

"If you see—"

"The three men you're hunting down, yep, I'll call you immediately."

"Thanks, I appreciate that." She paused. "But make sure you eat."

"I will." He produced a Mars bar.

She looked at Earle. He shrugged. They'd have to keep an eye on Andy, but right now, she was glad of his vigilance and his need to distract himself with work.

They headed into town, parked up near High Street, and walked to Aztec Pizza Parlour. It had been years since Shona had been there. The inside was a mixture of bright orange, yellow, and red, and pictures of what appeared to be crumbling temples lined the walls. Between the tables were huge plastic plants, giving a jungle appearance, albeit the leaves and fronds a little dusty.

"What are you having?" Earle asked as they took a window seat.

"Mushroom. You?"

"Ham and pineapple."

"Ah, controversial."

He chuckled. "Yeah, I've been told that before. Can't help it, I like the combo."

She smiled. It was good to hear him laugh and see a smidgen of tension slip away from his brow.

They ordered, and she stared out of the window, watching the early drinkers and restaurant-goers milling about. Soon the clubbers would be out, the girls tottering on heels and the blokes already a few drinks in before hitting the town.

She twirled a strand of hair around her finger. It seemed like a different life when that kind of evening had appealed. Now she liked to stay in on a Saturday night, or, at the most, a quiet meal out with family.

Her attention switched to Earle. They'd only been partners for a short while, but their connection had been swift. She already considered him a friend. She hoped he felt the same.

Their pizzas and sides arrived, along with cola.

"So what brought you into the force?" she asked.

"Always fancied it." He tore at a chunk of garlic bread. "I got a police outfit for Christmas one year, I was about six. Had little handcuffs and a plastic radio attached to the shirt."

She grinned. "That's kind of cute."

"Not often I get called cute." He bit into the bread, chewed, and swallowed. "What about you?"

She stared out of the window again. A group of girls were walking past, arms linked. They were chatting and laughing. "Two reasons."

"Go on."

"Them." She used her knife to point at the girls. "Girls. Women. Otherwise known as prey."

He raised his eyebrows.

"After what happened to me, I wanted to do something to stop it happening to others."

"I can understand that."

"But..." She leaned forward. "Mainly it was to catch the bastards who took me, Nicola, and Tina that night."

"That was your main motivation for years of training and study, not to mention beat hours?"

"Yep."

"Wow, that's a lot of determination and dedication."

"When you're feeling weak," she said, "it's when you have to be your strongest. I was lucky, my parents were supportive, and I harnessed all that anger, that hurt, and poured it into something positive—the DI status."

He nodded slowly.

"And now." She gestured outside again. "Now I'm so close, so ready…I can almost taste it."

"And if…I mean *when*…we get the bastards. What will you do?"

"You mean will I stop police work? Change my career?"

"I suppose."

"No, I love it now. This is who I am, a detective inspector."

"Good, it would be a waste of talent if you stopped."

"Ah, thanks, I appreciate that."

He grinned then glugged on his cola.

"But what I will do," she said, poking at a mushroom, "is start living again, maybe even…"

"What?"

"Go out more, take a holiday somewhere hot, date…"

"Date?"

"Perhaps. One step at a time, eh."

"We're a right pair, aren't we?"

"Maybe that's why we've been lumped together, Earle. Much as we look like polar opposites, we're actually very similar."

They finished up their pizza and watched twilight spread over High Street. The constant flow of people continued, and the lights above bars and restaurants flicked on.

Shona's phone rang. "Andy. Got something?"

"Yes, Samri Laghari and Vincent Thomas are walking south on High Street. They're currently beside Boots."

Her heart did a small flip. "Okay, thanks. We're in town; we'll see what they're up to. Let me know if you see the other one, Aran Barker."

"Will do…hang on."

"What?"

"I think they're aiming for Grapes Ahoy. They've just swerved in that direction."

"Cool, we'll go there now." She ended the call. "Andy spotted Samri and Vince, heading to the wine bar."

Earle stood. "Seems like we're due a glass of vino then. Or at least a non-alcoholic one."

Ten minutes later, they pushed out of the now-dark evening into the warmth of Grapes Ahoy. It was long and thin, the bar dominating the right-hand side, and fake grapes hung from the ceiling in an elaborate twist of plastic vines.

Already it was crowded; a press of people stood waiting to be served, and all the booths were full.

"Can you see them?" Shona asked.

Earle did a scan. "Nope, not yet."

"Let's move farther back."

"I'll grab us a drink."

"Good luck with that."

She entered deeper, squeezing past people and narrowly missing the contents of a glass of red that splashed her way. The rear end of the bar fanned out with extra seating with high vine-wrapped trellises, creating privacy between the tall tables shaped like wine barrels.

She spied a free table that had a couple of bar stools next to it and claimed the spot.

Once seated, she inspected the sea of faces around her.

There were several groups of girls knocking back Prosecco and wine, laughing and chatting as if they didn't have a care in the world. Their hair was fluffed up, lips glossed, and their outfits carefully coordinated.

A smidgen of envy caught in Shona's chest, but she pushed it away. She'd have that carefree feeling again soon, she was sure of it, and besides, envy was just an emotion that showed her what she wanted, a direction to go in, an ultimate aim.

There were blokes around, too, standing in groups of two or three, mostly with a beer rather than wine. Grapes Ahoy had always been a melting pot for guys and gals to meet. The amount of people in Ironash whose eyes had met beneath the plastic grapes had stopped being counted.

"Here, got you another cola, hope that's okay."

Earle was at her side.

"Yes, thanks." She took a sip as he sat. "See them?"

"No."

"Think Andy got it wrong?"

"It's a big place."

"And it's rammed."

Her focus was on the people around her, searching constantly for Samri's tall frame and dark greasy hair, and Aran's long, thin profile. It was as if her mind was in overdrive, working like a computer, checking and discounting.

Until her eyes connected with someone familiar.

A chiselled face with kind eyes and soft, dark hair.

Ben.

He stared at her, then his attention shifted to Earle.

"Shit," she muttered.

"What? You seen them?" Earle set his drink down and craned his neck in the direction she was looking.

"No... I..."

Ben was in front of her. "Hey, Shona."

"Ben." She swallowed.

Ben was staring at Earle with a mixture of confusion and hurt.

"It's nice to see you," she said.

"You, too, but unexpected. I thought you were working."

"I was. I am. I..." She pulled in a deep breath. "This is Earle. He's—"

"It's okay, you don't have to explain." He nodded at Earle. "Have a nice evening."

"Ben I..." Shit, he thought she'd turned him down to go out with Earle. "Wait."

But it was too late, he'd stepped back into the group of four blokes he was with and was glugging on his bottle of beer.

"Friend?" Earle asked.

"Kind of...yes, he is. I know him from karate."

"Ah, I see."

"He asked me out tonight, a date, I suppose, and I said I was working."

"Bugger, and now he's seen you here with me."

"But I am working and..." She flicked her finger between her and Earle. "And it's not as if..." Damn it, why was she so flustered? Why did she feel guilty when she had nothing to be guilty about?

"I know that, and you know that." He paused. "Maybe you should go and tell him we're partners, as in *work* partners."

She sighed and ran her hand over her hair. "No, I don't have to explain myself to him, or anyone. If he'd hung around longer, he could have had the explanation. His own fault if he feels..."

"Ditched."

"Yes, that's the word." She tutted. "Bugger."

"Hey." He rested his hand over hers. "Don't be so hard on yourself. From what you've said, you're out of the whole dating game. This kind of stuff happens all the time. You'll get the hang of it again."

"I suppose." She glanced at Ben once more.

He was staring their way, his focus on Earle's hand over hers.

Her phone rang. She pulled her hand from under Earle's and sat up straight as she answered it. "Andy?"

"They didn't go into the wine bar, or at least if they did it was only briefly."

"We're in here now, no sign."

"Nope, I spotted them loitering at the entrance a few minutes ago, chatting to some guy I'm currently running facial recognition on."

"It wasn't Aran Barker?"

"No, haven't seen him."

"Okay. And now where are they?"

"They're walking back along Haymarket in the direction of Samri's address."

"Alone?"

"Yes, just the two of them. I'll follow them as long as CCTV allows. They've got baseball caps on, by the way."

"Okay, and thanks, yes, do that. We'll swing by, make sure they made it home. Thanks, Andy." She ended the call. "They're not in town. Seems they called it a night."

"Really? I was sure they'd strike tonight." Earle frowned.

"Me, too."

A girl in a tight red dress came up to the table. She set a flier on the polished but slightly sticky surface. "Big night tomorrow. Don't miss out."

"What is it?" Shona picked up the leaflet.

"DJ Starz is at REVS, free entry before ten."

"On a Sunday?"

"Yep. See you there." She moved on to the next table.

Shona wafted the leaflet. "Here's a theory..."

"Go on." Earle folded his arms.

"They're saving themselves for tomorrow night. REVS, their preferred location of attack, is going to be packed."

Chapter Eleven

"But you were the last person to see her?" Beryl's husband, Brian, said down the phone. "When I went out with my mates, she said she was going to spend the evening with you."

"And yes, we did have dinner together, here, but I wasn't the last person to see her." Manfred hoped he'd injected enough concern into his voice.

"So who was?"

"The taxi driver. She ordered one from Valley Rides...at least I think it was that company, could have been A2B. I forget now. Oh dear, if only I could have seen which one it was. It might not have been either, I only heard the engine outside the house."

"What time was that?" He paused. "Shit, I'm so worried."

"About eleven, but it will be fine. She's probably gone to a friend's."

"Why on earth would she do that? She's got a perfectly good home. I know I come back a bit steaming from the dogs sometimes, but that doesn't usually bother her."

"I can understand why you're worried." He sighed again.

"Very. I called the police already."

Fuckity fuck.

Manfred's heart skipped a beat. "You did?" He gripped the phone.

"Yeah, right bunch of tosser, they are. Said that until she'd been gone twenty-four hours, they wouldn't do anything. Apparently she's not officially missing until then."

"But...oh, this is terrible. I feel so helpless."

It sounded as though Brian was pacing on a hard floor. "What kind of mood was she in, Mannie?"

Ah, he could use this angle. "To be honest..." He let a breath judder from his chest, as though holding in emotion. "Not good. Losing Terry and Fredrick has hit her hard, the way it has me, too, of course. We've all been friends for a long time. Such a shock, a terrible, terrible shock."

"And…?"

"And she was crying, a lot. Nothing I said seemed to comfort her. It was that real heart-wrenching sobbing…oh God, you don't think…that she'd do something stupid, do you?"

"I don't know what to think, Mannie, other than I'm desperately worried."

"I wish I could do something."

"Just try and remember everything she said, and if there's a clue to where she is, call me straight away."

"Of course."

"I'm going to ring the taxi companies, get to the bottom of this. My poor Beryl. If something has happened to her, I don't know how I'll go on."

He ended the call.

Manfred walked out into the back garden. He stood by the hot tub. The heater had flicked on as usual. It didn't smell so fresh today.

What the hell am I going to do with Beryl?

He could chop her up and feed her to Duke. She'd go in the freezer, limbs and organs in separate bags, and keep Duke going for months.

But not being able to see would make butchery nigh on impossible; Beryl wasn't a sausage casserole.

He could heave her out of the disgusting water and burn her at the end of the garden, behind the shed where it was private. Sure, her body would smell like a vile barbecue, but if he put a few steaks and pork chops on the grill at the same time, perhaps that would mask the meaty, salty-crackling scent.

Maybe he should dump the body. He could ram her into a suitcase—she was only little—take a taxi to the middle of nowhere, and dig a hole. Would a driver keep his mouth shut for an extra few quid? A spade and a heavy case to the countryside was hardly without suspicion.

Damn it. Why did she have to wind me up in the hot tub?

A simple death by drinking too much and stopping breathing would have sufficed. A handy ambulance would have disposed of the body for him, like with the others.

Ding-dong.

Duke barked. Manfred tensed. Who the hell was visiting? He hoped it wasn't Brian, or, heaven forbid, the nosey parker police again.

He flicked off the heater on the hot tub and went back inside. "Coming." He had to act normal, it was vital.

At the door, Duke beside him, he called through it. "Who is it?"

"It's me, Darrell. Let me in, Mannie."

Ah, it was the last of the Fucking Useless Four, how appropriate. And perhaps convenient.

"Hello, Darrell." He opened the door wide.

Duke's tail wagged against his leg.

"Shit, what the hell is happening? I just landed from Portugal, got a garbled message from Beryl, and now she's not answering her phone. I came straight here."

"Come in, come in." Manfred stepped aside.

Darrell rushed in, stress coming off him in waves and fizzing through the air. "Fuck, I need a drink. Was supposed to come back from holiday feeling all calm, ready to face the world, and now this…"

"I'll fix you a drink, go and sit in the living room." As far away from the hot tub as possible.

"Cheers, Mannie. I hope you don't mind me coming round like this…it's just…Terry and Fredrick. Poor buggers."

"It's a shock, and tragic, I know. I feel it, too. Let me fix these drinks." He walked to the cabinet, felt for the shape of the expensive Scotch, and held it up. "A splash of tonic with this?"

"You know me well, thanks."

"Just take a few deep breaths, relax. Don't want you keeling over, too."

Darrell blew out a puff of air. The chair back squeaked when he flopped against it.

Manfred found his way to the kitchen then set two crystal glasses on the worktop. He poured an inch of whisky into both, then took one outside. The sun shone down. A blackbird set off an alarm call as he walked past the buddleia. When he came to the shed, he pulled the door open and paused, visualising where everything was.

A high back shelf held paint cans from Colour Me Happy, oil, WD40, barbecue lighter fuel, and a bottle of antifreeze. The antifreeze was in a tall plastic bottle about the size of a plus-size washing-up liquid. Its main ingredient, ethylene glycol, was an odourless, syrupy, slightly sweet-tasting poison. All it would take was a few inches, and Darrell would be heading to Hell with his dickhead friends and disgusting Beryl.

If I've got one body to dispose of, might as well have two.

A sense of anticipation blustered through Manfred's veins. He was so near to fulfilling his revenge he could almost taste it.

He chuckled at 'taste it'. Chances were, Darrell wouldn't even notice the lethal addition to his Scotch.

He picked up the bottle and removed the childproof lid. Held it over the crystal glass.

A sudden movement behind him sent a rush of panic up his spine and over his scalp. His heart seemed to do an extra beat.

But it was just Duke, coming to see where he was.

"Shit, don't do that," Manfred muttered, quickly pouring so the glass was almost full. "You'll have *me* dropping down dead."

Duke snuffled about while Manfred returned the antifreeze to the shelf.

"Come on, boy. Let's go get this final job done."

Duke trotted beside him as he went to the kitchen—the constant companion, utterly trustworthy. Duke would never reveal Manfred's secrets.

"Alexa, play Beethoven's *Ninth Symphony*."

"Playing Beethoven *Symphony Number Nine* on Spotify."

The first string tones started up as Manfred walked to the living room, carefully holding the two glasses. "Here, yours is the full one. With the tonic."

"Thanks." Darrell took it. "What's this music?"

The tempo was ramping up.

"It's from *Clockwork Orange*, you seen that?"

"Ah, yeah, thought I recognised it." The chair creaked again. Darrell sitting back. Maybe crossing his legs, too.

Manfred also took a seat, on the sofa, where Terry had died.

"So what the fuck happened?" Darrell asked. "Sorry, I'm completely stunned. I mean, work tomorrow..." He took a big slug of his drink. "No Terry, no Fredrick."

And no farting, pooping Beryl either.

Manfred suppressed a grin, which was easy. His lips were so disfigured, no one knew if he was smiling anyway. "Horrendous, truly horrendous week, only comparable to when this happened." He pointed at his face. "Terry came round, we had a good chinwag, ate salmon, and then sitting right here, with a Scotch...yours okay, by the way? Need more tonic?"

"No, it's good, thanks." He drank, only quietly, but Manfred heard.

"Good. Terry he...he just keeled over, collapsed. It happened so fast. One minute he was talking, the next he was saying he was hot, that his chest hurt, and then nothing."

"That's awful."

"I did my best, called the ambulance, tried to loosen his clothing, check for a pulse and whatnot, but with my eyes..." He shook his head. "I wasn't much help."

"And when the ambulance arrived?"

"They tried, but it was futile. Huge heart attack, they think."

"He seemed so fit and well."

"Guess it goes to show."

Doesn't matter how fit you are if digoxin hits your cardiac muscle. Drink up, Darrell. Cheers and all that...

An excited swirl caught Manfred's stomach. Soon he'd have knocked off all of the Fucking Useless Four. He could hardly wait.

"And Fredrick? What happened to him?"

"That damn strawberry allergy, although he didn't have strawberries, of course, I was very careful about that. I left the packets out for him to check himself, because I can't, you know..." He wafted his hand near his glasses. "Said the ingredients were fine, then went into shock, couldn't breathe, collapsed."

"The very next night."

"I know...but he had come round because he knew I was upset, which was kind of him. Oh, but he shouldn't have. If he'd stayed away he'd be alive." Manfred bowed his head and feigned a sob.

"Hey, it's not your fault, mate. Accidents happen."

"I feel so responsible." He downed his drink, hoping Darrell would mimic him.

"This tonic is sweet."

"Is it? Sorry. I switched from Asda to Tesco home delivery, it's their own brand."

"That's okay, just a bit...different."

"Would you like something to eat?"

"No, I've been scoffing all week." He sighed. "Shit, I'm dreading tomorrow."

They sat in silence for a few minutes, listening to the rousing symphony coming from the kitchen.

"Got a bit of headache actually," Darrell said. "Might bother you for a sandwich, maybe I am hungry."

"I've got ham. You like that?"

"Thanks. That's really kind of you."

Manfred wasn't sure, but Darrell's speech had sounded a little slurred. Was the antifreeze kicking in already? Would be great if it was.

He went to the kitchen. "Alexa, volume down."

The music reduced a notch.

He found the bread, ham, and butter then set it on a board.

"Here you go, boy." He dropped a bit of ham to Duke.

"Shit. I feel like shit."

Darrell was behind him.

"What's up?" Manfred asked, holding the butter-laden knife over the bread.

"I just..." He sat with a bump. "My head's pounding, making me dizzy."

Oh yes, his speech is going. Good-o.

"You still want this ham sandwich?" Manfred buttered it anyway. He was getting hungry. Murder did that to a person. Or so he'd discovered.

"What...what are you doing?" Darrell asked.

"I'm making you this—"

He was interrupted by an enormous heaving sound, then splashing.

"Shit!" Manfred spun around.

Darrell must have puked all over the kitchen floor. He groaned and it sounded like he lolled against the table, ramming it into the wall.

"Darrell!" Manfred cried. Fuck it. He'd vomited the poison back up. Would it still work? "What's the matter?"

"I'm sick...I'm not well...the same as..." He paused.

Manfred could almost hear the cogs of his mind working.

"The same as Terry and Fredrick...what have you done to me? What did you do to *them*?"

"Nothing. Do you want me to call a doctor? An ambulance?"

Darrell groaned.

"Here, drink up your Scotch, that will make you feel better." Manfred located the glass and moved it to where he guessed Darrell was slumped.

Suddenly it was swiped violently from his hand. It crashed to the floor then smashed, the glass tinkling in a hundred different directions.

Manfred stepped back, shock gripping him.

Duke barked.

"You...you've done this, Mannie. What was in...that drink?"

"Nothing untoward." Manfred wound his hands together. "I promise."

"Yes...there was..." He groaned again, as though his stomach was hurting. "I can take a Scotch without this happening. And Terry, Fredrick...what did you do to them?"

"Nothing, I—"

"Don't lie, Mannie, you ugly old git, you've poisoned me. You poisoned them, too."

Manfred was shocked at Darrell's change of tone. He'd always been such an affable young fellow, if a little shallow.

"I'm going to get you for this," Darrell slurred. "Tell the police what you've done."

"I haven't done anything."

Darrell thumped his fist on the table, the sound exploding around the room, competing with the dramatic music. "I know you have."

Manfred puffed up his chest and reached for the knife again. It wasn't particularly sharp, but sharp enough if he needed to defend himself. "Okay."

"What the hell does 'okay' mean?" Darrell sounded weak—talking was energy-sapping.

Good, he's dying.

"Okay, I killed them, too." There, he'd said it. "Right here, in my home."

"But...why? Why the fuck would you do that?"

"Why? Why?" He waggled the knife. "Because you fucking useless four didn't put that aerosol together properly. It was your fault, all of you that it exploded, taking away my sight, my face, and the rest of my life."

"It was an accident, no one was to blame."

"Someone is always to blame—in this case, four people."

"So you decided to...kill us? Poison us?"

"Yes, well, not Beryl, but you blokes, yes."

"But..." He groaned. "That's evil, Mannie. I thought..."

"That I was a nice old guy? You thought wrong." He took a step closer. How easy would it be to stab someone in his dark world? He'd have a go.

"No, stop." Darrell retched. "No, please."

The music was bugging, and it wasn't helping Manfred judge where his victim was. "Alexa, music off."

"Alexa...call the police!"

"What...?" Manfred was shocked.

"Alexa, call the police now. To this address," Darrell yelled. "54 Drover Road."

"Are you sure you want to call the police as an emergency?"

"Yes," Darrell shouted. "Alexa, call the police. Tell them that Manfred Napier is trying to murder me. That he's murdered two other men."

"Connecting to local emergency services."

"No..." Manfred lunged forward but came into contact with nothing but the table and the wall. Darrell had slid from harm. "You bastard."

"You're mad," Darrell shouted from somewhere near the door. "Fucking mad."

Manfred rushed to the sound of his voice, knife raised. He jabbed it down and forward. A huge jolt went up his arm to his shoulder and neck as he collided with the wall.

"You fucker, I'll tell them what you've done, what you told me. How you've murdered people."

"Come here." Manfred was manic. Thoughts and rage spun in his head, in his body. Every beat of his heart pulsed red-hot panic and fury into his veins.

He'd been so close, now Darrell was getting away.

Darrell was going to ruin everything.

And so was his super-duper, connected, all-listening Alexa.

Bitch.

Chapter Twelve

"Strange coincidence, DI," Andy said down the phone.

"Go on..." Shona stood peeling potatoes with her mother. Sunday roast was a tradition not to be missed in the Williams' household.

"Just had an emergency call, via Alexa, from Manfred Napier's house."

"What?"

"Yeah, we've only ever had a couple of them—new connected service that's being rolled out. I've sent some uniforms but thought you'd want to know as you gave me his name yesterday to run through the system."

"Thanks." She set down the knife. "I'll pop round, it's not far. Poor old guy knows me. Might be easier on him if it's a voice he recognises, you know, if he's got some kind of incident going on."

"Okay, ma'am, sorry to bother you on a Sunday."

"It's no bother, and you're in the office again?"

He sighed. "Best place for me at the moment."

"Well, you'll have to take this time back, when there's something you want to do, a beach to go lie on maybe."

"I will. Want me to call DS Montague?"

"No, I'll do that on the way. Thanks." She ended the call and turned to her mother. "I have to pop out for a while, work thing."

"No problem, dear." She cracked an egg into a bowl.

"I'll be back before dinner, though."

Five minutes later, Shona was driving towards Manfred Napier's house. She hoped he hadn't come to any harm; he'd had enough of his fair share of shitty luck.

She hit dial on Earle's number.

"Good morning," he said after two rings. "I hope you're not going to disturb me from my batch baking. Got a tray of chocolate brownies in the oven and a seriously good carrot cake just about to go in."

"Hopefully not. Just wanted to let you know I'm heading to Manfred Napier's. There's been an emergency call from there."

"Want me to meet you?"

"No, you stay there with your pinny on." She giggled at the image.

"It's a very manly pinny, I'll have you know."

"I'm sure it is." She indicated right. "Uniforms are on the way. Just thought that since he's blind he might like a familiar voice if he's had a break-in or something."

"Good thinking. We still on for later?"

"Yes, definitely. See you then."

"I'll pick you up, about eight."

"Perfect."

She hit 'end call' and swung onto the road Mr Napier lived on. There were no marked cars—she'd beaten uniform.

Quickly, she pulled up outside the cute little bungalow. All was quiet with the front door closed.

With her flat shoes silent, she moved swiftly to the front door. She stood and listened.

"You bastard!"

"Just hurry up and die, will you."

What the fuck?

She banged on the door. "Police, open up!"

The dog barked—loud, excitable woofs.

"Police. Open up now." She shoved at the door, but it was locked shut. "Damn it." She scanned the road. Where the hell was backup? Something was clearly going down.

A scrabble on the other side of the door, as if someone was there, dragging on it.

"Open up before we smash it down," she said.

"Hang...on..." A weak voice.

Impatience clawed at her.

And then it opened, just an inch.

She curled her fingers around it and eased it ajar, aware she was pushing against a dead weight. When she could see enough, she realised it was a slumped male body.

"Shit." She glanced up the hallway. Empty. Not even the dog.

The man blocking her way appeared to be losing consciousness. She squeezed in and crouched beside him, searching for obvious wounds.

Nothing.

"What's your name?" she asked.

"He...he did this..."

"Who did?" She reached for her phone.

"Manfred, he..."

"What?" She called the office. Andy picked up. "We need an ambulance at Manfred Napier's address, now!"

"On it."

The man on the floor, mid-thirties, tanned, chiselled jawline, gripped her t-shirt. "He did it, Mannie, he's poisoned me...he poisoned the others, too."

"What?" Was she hearing right? The poor old blind guy had been on a killing spree? "He poisoned Terry Smith and Fredrick Deans?"

"Yes. He admitted it." He groaned, drawing his knees up to his belly. "Help me. Please."

"An ambulance is on the way? Where is Mr Napier now?"

"I...I don't know..." His eyes rolled back. A gurgle bubbled up from his throat.

"Shit." She looked over her shoulder.

The dog was there now, standing in the kitchen doorway, wagging its tail, panting.

"Where's your master, eh?" She stood. In the distance, a faint siren filtered towards her. "Show me where he is."

She glanced at the man on the floor. There was nothing she could do for him. He needed paramedics. But she could find Manfred Napier, make sure he didn't get away.

How far can a blind man get?

Shona wasn't prepared to find out. She'd heard his voice, she was sure, when she'd been outside the door, so he was still around, so was his guide dog.

She made her way down the hallway, pausing to look in a bedroom on her right. A woman's red jacket and matching handbag sat side by side on a chair in the corner. There appeared to be a pile of clothes beside it—flowery dress and underwear.

Shona frowned. Manfred had said he lived alone. Who did they belong to? A girlfriend perhaps? And if so, where was she?

A sense of urgency gripped her. If he had a seeing accomplice, he could be taking off fast.

With the dog coiling around her legs, she went into the living room. The sun was just spilling through the bay window, a streak of light dancing with dust motes. The door to a drink's cabinet was open, one of those pull-down ones, and a bottle of Scottish whisky sat with the lid off. Red checked cushions were dented on the sofa and in a chair.

Moving on, she got to the kitchen. Glass covered the floor, and the smell of whisky was strong. A dinner knife, coated in butter, sat amongst the shards, and a half-made sandwich lay on a breadboard by the sink. "Mr Napier?"

No answer.

The dog picked its way around the glass, paused to sniff the knife, then went out through the open back door.

"Very sensible," she muttered, "before you cut your paws." She followed him out into the long, thin back garden. The hot tub to her right needed a clean by the smell of it. Beyond that was a shed.

She studied the perimeter. It was a well-enclosed garden, private, too, owing to the fact it was surrounded by one-storey properties.

The dog cocked its leg against a barbecue, then wandered over to her.

She tickled his soft, silky head. The sirens were loud now, emergency services seconds away. Whatever the guy by the door had ingested was nasty, he needed treatment quick.

Let's hope they're quick enough.

"Where your master? Can you show me?"

The dog looked up at her with big, chocolate-brown eyes. They brimmed with intelligence.

"Where is he? Go find..."

The dog turned away, lolloped along to the shed.

Her belly tensed. Was he hiding in there?

It would have been sensible to wait for backup, she knew that, but what harm could Manfred do her? She had every advantage over him. But he might not have done anything wrong at all. Innocent until proven guilty.

But she didn't believe herself with that last thought. There'd been too many deaths at this address, and now a poisoning. Manfred Napier was the common denominator.

The dog stopped by the shed and turned to her.

"Good boy," she said, moving to his side. But damn, that hot tub hummed. Bloody environmental hazard, that was what it was.

Very quietly, she lifted the latch on the shed door.

It creaked open, and a spider dropped down on its web, dangling before her. She batted it out of the way.

Inside it was dusty but neat. A lawn mower, a spade and rake, a bunch of hot tub cleaning tablets and liquid. On a shelf sat oil, antifreeze, and a whole range of paints.

But there was no Manfred Napier. No one hiding out.

"Bloody hell," she muttered. Maybe he had escaped with help of a woman.

She shut the door and stepped out into the garden again. A set of pavers led a path around the shed.

The dog stepped along them.

A sudden tension seized her. She recognised it. A feeling she'd had many times. She was close, so close to him.

"Mr Napier," she said, coiling a lock of hair around her finger. "This is DI Williams, we met the other day."

Nothing.

"We need to talk." She kept her focus on the dog. "Someone called the police from your Alexa device."

The dog was standing parallel to the end of the shed, head slightly up and tail wagging.

Bingo.

She walked on the grass, silently. Her breaths were coming in short, shallow inhales. Adrenaline spiked in her system. She was ready to fight...flight wasn't an option.

Peering around the end of the shed, the dog beside her legs, she swallowed and flexed and un-flexed her fingers.

Manfred Napier stood rod straight, chin tilted, dark glasses on and hands pressed in a prayer position. His twisted lips were trembling, and his shirt was untucked on one side.

"Mr Napier, do you remember me?" she asked.

He nodded.

"Can you tell me who called the emergency services?"

"It was a mistake?" His voice was hoarse, as though he'd been shouting.

"I don't think so. There's someone in your hallway in a lot of pain and claiming to have been poisoned."

"He's lying."

She glanced to her right. A uniformed officer was stepping out of the kitchen. The dog trotted over to him, tail bobbing from side to side.

"Why would he lie, Mr Napier?"

"Because he's a useless fucker, that's why. That's all they do is lie."

She frowned. "Who is they?"

"All of them."

The uniform came to her side. She held up her finger to her mouth. He nodded.

"Can you tell me whose clothes are in your bedroom?"

"Mine." Manfred huffed.

"No, the woman's clothes."

"What?" His mouth fell open.

"On the chair by the window. There are female clothes and a handbag. I thought you lived alone."

"I do. I...a girlfriend, she popped by."

"Where is she now?"

"I...I don't know. She went, late last night."

"Without her clothes? Her bag?"

"She didn't need them. She had spare."

The uniform had his notepad out and was writing.

Excellent.

"Can you tell me her name?"

"Er...yes, it's Beryl Bint, but..."

"But what?"

Sweat peppered his scarred brow, and he twisted his hands together. "But you can't tell her husband."

"Ah, like that, is it? Okay, I understand the need for discretion, but we will need to speak to her."

"Why? Why do you need to talk to her?"

"Because you've had some accusations made against you, Mr Napier. If there's someone who can prove your innocence, you're going to need them."

"She's gone."

"What do you mean?" Shona frowned.

"Gone, missing..."

"Missing?" She shared a look with the uniform, a tall, dark-haired young man.

He shrugged and downturned his mouth.

"What do you mean 'missing'?" she asked again.

"Her husband called, said she hadn't got home after she'd popped round to see me."

"So he knows you two are..."

"No!" He gritted his teeth. Spittle had collected at the corners of his mouth. "Of course not."

"But her clothes are here?"

Suddenly he lunged forward, arms spread, as if trying to grab her. His face was bright red, and her reflection glinted in his dark glasses.

She batted his right arm out of the way and swept his feet from under him. Two swift moves that had him hitting the lawn chest first and the air rushing from his lungs.

"You bitch," he yelled.

The uniform dropped to his knees, cuffs at the ready. He grabbed Manfred's arms and hoisted them around his back.

Manfred squirmed and kicked, bashed his forehead onto the grass. "Do what you want with me, I've fulfilled my mission, I have sought my revenge."

"Revenge for what?" she asked as the familiar metallic sound of cuffs locking gave her a sense of satisfaction.

"For doing this to me, taking away everything, my life, for turning me into a monster."

Another uniform appeared and helped the first haul Manfred to his feet.

"You are under arrest on suspicion of murder," Shona said. "You have the right to remain silent. You do not have to say anything, but it may harm your defence if you fail to mention when questioned, something you later rely on in court. Anything you do say may be used as evidence."

"Is he dead? Is the fourth one dead? He should be." His madness infused every word, every syllable.

"Paramedics are just loading him onto the ambulance," the second uniform said.

"Good." She pointed to Manfred. "Get him down to the station."

"Yes, ma'am."

"And take the dog. We'll call the RSPCA or whoever to come and take him. Can't imagine the poor thing will want a life behind bars." She scratched the dog behind the ears. "In fact, he'd be more suited to police work."

"Duke, no, not my Duke. I have to have him with me."

"You should have thought of that," the first uniform said, yanking Manfred forward.

Shona placed her hands on her hips. Manfred had mentioned four victims. Yes, she knew three, the men, but who was the fourth?

It could only be the woman, Beryl Bint.

A nasty niff rose again, from the hot tub. She stared at it.

Oh no.

Her stomach tightened, apprehension once more sending adrenaline into her system.

Is the smell...?

It wasn't a theory she wanted to prove, but she had no choice, she had to check. She had to lift the lid, literally.

She stepped up to it. The heater was chugging. Trying to breathe shallowly, she found a tissue in her pocket and used it to undo the clips.

The stink increased, and as she moved back the covering, she had to hold down a rush of bile. She ballooned her cheeks and held her breath.

Floating in the disgusting hut tub water was a woman in a black swimsuit. Facedown. Her grey hair spread out, and her pale shoulders hunched forward.

"Shit." Shona dragged her to the edge and flipped her over, just in case there was a chance she was alive.

But no, her skin was crinkled, her reddened eyes stared straight ahead, and her lips were blue.

"You must be Beryl Bint." Shona removed her hand from the rank water. "I'm so sorry this happened to you." She sighed then called over her shoulder. "Can I have some help out here?"

A uniformed police officer appeared at her side. "Ah, shit, that's not good." He pinched his nose. "Smells bad, too."

"Yes, I'm going to wash my hands. Can you organise SOCO to get out here and the photographer. Also get a log started, and everyone needs suiting up."

"Yes, ma'am." He pulled out his phone. "Anything else?"

"Yes." She pointed at the kitchen. "Alexa, get that bagged up as evidence and dropped off at the station. Give it to Sergeant Andy Pierce."

"Yes, ma'am." He paused. "If you don't mind me asking, why?"

"Of course I don't mind. Manfred Napier has add-ons to his assistant programme, because of his blind status: It can control the lights, house temperature and that, and it can call the emergency services."

"Okay." He appeared confused.

"And I want to know what else he's been asking her to do, and if some of his conversations have been recorded without him knowing we need to listen to them."

His eyes widened. "Really. Private conversations are listened to?"

"Yes, really, and if there's anything incriminating, well, we can use it."

"Alexa as a witness?" He shook his head.

"An independent witness, very reliable. A case in the US just committed a man for murder on her evidence." She held up her hands. "I need to wash...that water is crappy."

Chapter Thirteen

"Hey, what's going down?" Earle strode into the office.

"Like I said on the phone, I've brought Manfred Napier in on charges of murder and attempted murder."

"Bloody hell. And we discounted him as a harmless old blind bloke."

She wasn't proud of that fact. "Just goes to show."

"Andy's in again?" He nodded in the direction of Andy's desk.

"So are we, I suppose." She shrugged. "Did you get the cakes out of the oven?"

"Yeah, cakes are all fine." He smiled. "Are we questioning Napier now?"

"Yes, let's get it over with, then we can concentrate on REVS tonight."

"No rest for the wicked, right."

"Tell me about it."

They headed down to the interrogation rooms. Manfred had been seated, with his dog, Duke, at a table in room four. A uniform stood outside, and when they entered, he came in and stood by the door.

"Mr Napier, it's DI Williams and DS Montague, you've met us both before."

He stared straight ahead, though the dog stood and wagged his tail. He wore a reflective yellow jacket.

Shona and Earle took seats opposite Manfred. Earle pressed 'start' on the tape recorder.

Shona repeated who was in the room for the benefit of the recording and stated the date and time. "Mr Napier," she went on, "do you understand why you have been arrested?"

"I do." He pressed his puffy lips together.

"Three people are dead, each death happened on your property' and you are the main suspect."

"The fourth?"

"Darrell Dawkins is in hospital in a critical condition." She knotted her hands on the desk. "What did you give him?"

"No comment."

Shona wasn't too worried, they'd soon find out.

"We found the body of Beryl Bint in your hot tub. Can you tell me what happened?"

"No comment."

She sighed.

"And Terry Smith and Fredrick Deans... We at first thought their deaths were due to natural causes, but now we have reason to believe you played a part in their demise."

"No comment."

"What did you mean..." she glanced at her notebook, "by 'I've fulfilled my mission, I have sought my revenge'?"

"No comment."

"Mr Napier." She sighed. "This isn't getting us very far."

"I want a solicitor."

She looked at Earle and shook her head. This was a waste of time. She stood. "Quite honestly, Mr Napier, I think you need one. And just so you know, we've taken your Alexa device as evidence."

He pulled a face, the right side of his scarred check contracting. "What?"

"It's an easy enough task for us to find out what you've been asking her over the last few days, as well as identify conversations you've had within her recording range."

"She doesn't listen in...that's impossible. You can't do that. That's spying. The privacy of my own home...you can't." He banged his fist on the table. "That's a violation of my human rights."

"When you start poisoning people, you have to accept you'll be investigated and some rights will evaporate." Shona stroked the dog again, his tail flicking from side to side as he gazed up at her with trusting eyes. She straightened and turned to the uniform "Is someone coming to pick the dog up?"

"Yes, ma'am. Within the hour."

"Good, the less time he's behind bars the better, but as for his owner, I think we'll be looking at a long stretch. The evidence is pretty damning."

* * * *

Shona enjoyed a Sunday roast and all the trimmings as well as her parents' company. It was nice to be home with familiar tastes, scents, and surroundings. Topped with getting another madman—another serial killer—behind bars, she was feeling good.

As good as she ever could while three evil men still walked free on the streets of Ironash.

But that was all going to change soon. Very soon. She was determined to make that happen.

At eight o'clock, as planned, Earle pulled up outside. When she walked to the door—leather trousers, white blouse, and patent black flat shoes—her father followed her.

"Shona."

"Yes, Dad."

"Be...you know...careful."

"I'm not seventeen anymore."

"No, of course not, but you're still my little girl. It's an ugly big world out there."

"Tell me about it. But I've got tools to protect myself now, and I'm a DI."

"I know, and I'm grateful for that, but even so, you need me, just call, I'm not that old."

She laughed. "Got you on speed dial."

He glanced out of the window by the front door. "So that's your new partner, eh?"

"Earle, yes, he's great. I got lucky."

"I'm glad you feel that way. A partner you click with is important. Especially if you're going to be sticking around for a while." He raised his eyebrows questioningly.

"I am. If you'll have me."

"Well..." He scratched his chin, pretended to think about it. "I suppose we could put up with you."

She laughed and shoved her phone, ID, and a twenty into her pockets. "I'll see you later, hopefully with news."

He nodded. "Hopefully."

She slipped out into the warm evening and jogged down the path to Earle's car.

"Ready for action?" he asked when she climbed in.

"You bet." She fastened her seat belt.

As he pulled away, a roll of nerves hit her stomach. This would be her first time in REVS since *that* night. She wasn't looking forward to being in those familiar surroundings. They held too many memories, or rather, not enough.

"Andy's still in the office," Earle said.

"Bloody hell, I hope he's had a Sunday roast since I last spoke to him."

"Told me he went to the carvery. Not sure I believe him, though."

"He really is having a tough time." She checked her red lipstick in the mirror on the sun visor. "Wish I could do more."

"You're letting him work. Seems distraction therapy is what he needs, so I suppose that's something."

"True. I'll call him." She flicked the sun visor up and grabbed her phone. "Hey, Andy, how are you doing?"

"All good. You really think the three amigos are going to be out and about tonight?"

"Yes, I do. Historically, attacks happen over this weekend, though I still can't work out why. There was nothing last night, but with the big-shot DJ playing at REVS tonight, I'd put money on them slipping a few roofies to some unsuspecting girls."

"Okay, well, I've got eyes on High Street CCTV and an alert on ANPR for Samri Laghari's and Aran Barker's vehicles."

"Perfect. Can you send me through any images we have of the three of them? I'll flash them to the bouncers, get those guys on side, too."

"I'm on it."

"Thanks, speak later."

They drove into the town, found a parking space just off High Street, then wandered towards REVS.

"Looking smart, partner," Shona said, taking in Earle's tight black jeans and short-sleeved grey shirt.

"Didn't want to stand out as a copper."

"Well, I don't think you'll do that, but you'll still stand out."

"I will?" He frowned.

"Yes." She laughed. "You're a six-foot-plus handsome black guy, of course you'll stand out."

He shrugged. "Thanks for the compliment, I think."

"Just use that height to eyeball the crowd, okay."

"That's my plan."

They arrived at the entrance. Two meaty-shouldered bouncers were hanging around the doorway.

Shona revealed her ID. "Hello, fellas, we're going to be around tonight."

"Got a problem?" one asked in a deep voice.

"There's a few people of interest. If you see them, can you let us know?" She found the three images Andy had sent through.

They both studied them.

"Seen these blokes before?" she asked.

"Maybe that one, with the big ears."

"Good, okay. If you spot him or the others, this is my number." She waited while they both keyed it in. "Call straight away. These are not fine upstanding citizens, and if they're here, they're up to no good."

"You want us to pin them down, till you arrive?"

"And risk you getting charged with assault? No, leave the pinning down to us. A call will do. Let them into the club, then let me know, no drama." She pointed to her eyes with her index and middle finger. "This is what I need, you to be observant, watch, nothing more for now."

"We're on it. Expecting it to be busy, though. This place was practically empty last night. Everyone's saving it up for tonight, what with that fancy-pants DJ in town."

"That's what we thought." She gestured to the door. "We'll just go in."

"Of course."

She glanced up at the CCTV monitor angled down at the entrance. Andy would be watching through it; he'd know where they were.

A set of red-carpeted steps led to a ticket booth. Shona kept her ID out and flashed it at the girl behind the glass.

She raised her eyebrows a fraction and waved them in but didn't pause chewing her gum.

Shona's heart rate was picking up with each step she took deeper into REVS. She was glad she'd worn flats, not just in case she needed to run, but also because her knees felt a little weak, a bit wobbly.

The last time I was here...

No, don't think like that.

This is the present, not the past, this is what I have control over. This is what counts.

At the archway that led into the bar area, dance floor, and stage, she paused.

There were already a lot of people milling around. The DJ's equipment had been set up, but there was no one mixing. The bar staff were busy with a one deep spread of customers.

"Want a cola?" Earle asked.

"We should look the part, I suppose."

"You go find a seat, I'll get them."

"Okay, thanks."

He walked away, and she found herself staring up at the spotlights directed over the dance floor.

A sudden image of her, Nicola, and Tina dancing, spinning each other around, laughing, came to her mind. They'd been so young, so innocent...so naïve.

"Hi, love, want a drink?"

A stocky man with a beard stood to her right.

"No, thanks. My friend is getting me one." She pointed at Earle.

He followed her line of sight.

"The big one," she said. "That's my friend."

"Ah, okay, you have a nice night." He walked away.

Truth was, she was probably more deadly than Earle, but she'd keep that to herself.

Gathering her courage, she walked towards the dance floor. Instead of going over it and interrupting the handful of groovers, she made her way to the booths that lined the left-hand wall.

For some reason, she found herself drawn to the very one she'd shared with Nicola and Tina that night.

It was empty.

She slid into it, her trousers gliding on the red bench. A fake candle was set on the table. Taking a deep breath, she settled back. Now it was time to watch and wait. She'd done that often enough in London, and it had been ingrained in her to be patient at stakeouts.

But this is different.
This is personal.

Earle appeared and sat opposite her. He placed two drinks down.

"Thanks." She took a sip, glad of the cool, sweet liquid.

"Listen, I know this is personal," he said, "but if you can, stay in DI mode."

She nodded; he'd summed up her thoughts. "I know I have to. It's hard." She patted the bench. "This is where we sat."

"Which we'll take as a good sign—from here we'll see them."

"What if they see us? Samri will recognise me from last week. I knocked him to the floor and then hauled his arse down the station."

"I don't think he will. Then you had your hair up, no makeup. Tonight, your appearance is different what with the lipstick and..." he made a fluffing motion around his head, "the hair, and don't forget you're out of context. He won't be expecting a policewoman to be here."

"Just prey."

"Yeah. Just prey." He scanned the bar area. "It's filling up quickly."

"Good." She took another few gulps of drink. "The sooner we nail them the better."

"Relax."

"I'm trying." She blew out a breath.

"DI mode."

She nodded. "I'm on it. Let's sit and watch. Shout if you see any of them."

For the next hour, Shona scanned the clubbers arriving, getting drinks, then claiming small areas of territory around the dance floor and in the booths. The girls were dressed in sparkly, barely there dresses and heels that should come with 'ankle-breaker' warnings.

But despite careful observations, neither Samri, Vince, or Aran had shown up.

"Damn it," she muttered when a cheer blasted through the place.

The DJ had taken to the stage.

"Where are they?"

"The night is young," Earle said. "Youngsters go out late these days, stay in first for drinks."

"I suppose." Her phone vibrated. Andy. "Hey, got something?"

"Yes, Samri's van just pulled up two streets away. All three of our guys got out and are heading in your direction."

"Shit, really? Thanks. Stay in touch." She ended the call. "Earle, the eagle has landed."

"Good."

The music was blasting out, deep pulses that seemed to vibrate through to her heart. She finished her drink and kept her attention in the direction of the entrance. It was hard to see, though. The bar was packed, the crush of people taking up all the space.

"It's too busy," she muttered.

Earle didn't seem to hear her.

Her phone rang. "Hello."

"It's Ted, bouncer. Your three blokes just walked in."

"Thanks, keep vigilant. If you see them leave, I need to know." She ended the call and tapped Earle's arm. "They're here!"

"Want me to circulate?"

"Yes, good idea." She nodded.

He slid from the booth and into the swarm of people all clambering to get near the stage.

She craned her neck, desperate to see Samri and his revolting friends.

Suddenly the lights went out. Blackness. Silence. A shot of adrenaline spiked into her system.

"Can you handle that?" DJ Starz boomed. "Can you handle nothing?"

"No!" the crowd yelled.

"Are you numb?"

"No!" The roar was deafening.

"Good, because now it's time to parrrrrty!"

Once again the thumping tune thundered through the air. The lights came back on, strobes flashing and blinking.

Shona struggled to spot Earle but eventually found him on the other side of the dance floor. And was that Samri?

A tall male, greasy black hair, stood with his back to her, but as soon as she focused, he'd gone, swallowed by the rush of people now bouncing up and down to the beat.

"This is madness," she muttered. A creepy old alley would have been a much better stakeout, any day.

A group of girls tumbled up to her table, one spilling her drink over her wrist. "Hey, can you watch these, we're going to dance?"

"No problem." Shona smiled. "But if I'm not here when you get back, don't drink them."

One of them shrugged and turned, and the others followed, linking arms, their long legs tottering into the gaggle of dancers.

Shona watched them for several minutes, eyeing up who was around them, near them. It was as if her brain was programmed to spot Samri, Aran, and Vince. She'd see someone, dismiss them, see someone...

And then she spotted Aran. His long face, pokey-out ears a giveaway. He was talking to a man she didn't recognise as one of the others.

She stood, struggled to watch him while she looked for Samri and Vince.

"Hey, are you...yes, Shona Williams, well I'll be blowed!"

A woman appeared in front of her, the lights bouncing off her long, curly red hair.

"Bethany Taylor?" Shona raised her eyebrows. It had been years since she'd seen her old school friend.

"Bloody hell, you look great." Bethany dragged her into a hug.

Shona bristled, her limbs tensed, and her jaw tightened. She didn't return the hug.

"Oh my God! Wait till I tell Melanie you're back. You *are* back, aren't you?" She released Shona and slid onto the seat, blocking Shona's view.

"Er...yes, I am." A weird sense of reversing time washed through her. She was in Mr Richardson's English class. Her and Bethany sitting at the back of the room, dissecting *Pride and Prejudice* and wishing for their very own Mr Darcy.

"It's so good to see you, we must catch up over lunch." Bethany grinned, a familiar smile, a familiar face. "I know it was..." The smile slipped. "Hard after...you know, and then you went away, and Tina and Nicola." She frowned, clearly worried she'd said too much.

"It was hard." Shona nodded. "Really hard, and it still is." She glanced over Bethany's shoulder, hunting for Aran again.

"Listen, let's swap numbers, so we can talk properly, it's crazy in here."

Shona opened up a new contact screen on her phone. All the time she was tapping Bethany's number in, she was twitching with the need to study the dance floor and the men around it, watching the girls.

"It really is so nice to see you," Bethany shout-said. "Are you here alone?"

"No, with a friend."

"Who? Anyone I know?"

"I doubt it." She stood. "I really should go and find him."

"Didn't you go off and do your police training?" Bethany also stood. "That's what I heard."

She nodded. "Yes, and I really must go." She held up her phone. "But call me, I'd love to do lunch." As she'd said it, she realised she would. Bethany was nice, always had been. Maybe theirs was a friendship that could be resurrected. "These drinks belong to some girls dancing. Can you watch them?"

"Of course." Bethany sat back down. "Glad of the booth if you've finished with it. I'm here with my cousins, they're visiting especially to see DJ Starz."

"Good, enjoy yourselves." Shona's phone rang, and she stepped away. "Andy?"

"It's kicking off at the front, some kind of brawl. Both bouncers are involved. Not looking like fun."

"Uniform there?"

"Not yet, I've just sent a couple."

"Good."

"Shit...hang on."

"What?"

"The three suspects...fuck...they're leaving," Andy said. "I'm sure it's them, baseball caps again."

A wave of nausea gripped her belly. "Alone?"

"No." His voice deepened. "There's three girls with them, and by the way they're staggering, almost being dragged along, I'd say they're really fucking out of it."

Chapter Fourteen

"We have to intercept," Shona said. She'd never envisaged it getting this far. She'd wanted to catch them slipping the drugs and then attempting to make off with their victims, not actually get out of the club.

"Ah crap," Andy said. "REV's CCTV's just given out."

"What? How the hell could it?" Shona pushed through the crowd, heading for the entrance. The crush of people was insane, but rather than getting claustrophobic as she squeezed through the hot bodies, her sense of urgency cranked up. "Out of the way."

"I'm going to check on the van," Andy said, "follow it on camera if needs be."

"Don't take your eyes off it, and get more uniforms here, fast. I do not want that van driving away." She hung up and scrolled to Earle's number. But just as she found it, she was jostled to the right, her foot caught on someone else's, and she was knocked to her knees. "Shit."

One hand slapped on the floor. With the other she kept a protective grip on her phone. Someone walked past her, their knee knocking her temple. "Damn it."

She scrabbled to stand; it was as if she were invisible down there. A rise of panic squeezed her chest.

"Hey, lady, you okay?"

She was hauled upwards.

A young man, glasses, floppy brown hair, held her arm.

"Yes, thanks."

"You sure? You went down hard." He frowned.

"Absolutely." She felt rude but pushed past him, clamping her phone to her ear. "Earle, get your arse outside. They've just taken off with three girls, drugged by the sounds of it."

"Damn it. On my way."

She continued to try to elbow through the crowd. It was no good, it was taking too long. She delved into her pocket, pulled out her ID, and held it forward. "Police, out of the way, now." She used her best authoritative tone. "Police, let me through."

The crowd parted, not perfectly, no Moses and the Red Sea, but her way was easier as people glanced at the ID and then her and shifted to one side.

Eventually, she rushed up the steps to the foyer.

Earle was close behind her.

"Your CCTV is out!" Shona banged her hand on the sill of the ticket booth. "Get it fixed!"

"What? An engineer was here this afternoon."

Shona frowned. "Well, he didn't do a very good job on it. I want it working again, fast." She rushed to the big double doors that were wide open.

The two bouncers were caught up with a couple of drunk guys hurling abuse at each other. One had a streak of blood from his brow to his cheek, and he was slamming his hand into his fist as another bloke held him back. The biggest of the two bouncers stood in the middle of the fray, his arms out, palms up.

"Calm the fuck down or you'll be heading to the nick."

Another man, beefy tattooed arms, rushed forward, a primal yell coming from his mouth as he held up a bottle. He caught the attention of the second bouncer who sprang on him and wrestled him to the ground.

"Bollocks," Earle muttered.

"We haven't got time." Shona had her phone by her ear. "Andy, did you see which direction they were heading in?"

"Yes, ma'am, towards the van, I think, so right when you come out of REVS."

"Has the van moved?"

"No, it's still there on Tanner's Walk."

"Good." She finished the call. "Earle, this way."

She set off at a run, going east on High Street. She knew where Tanner's Walk was, her mum used to go to the hairdressers there.

Earle was with her, his footsteps slapping down.

Her heart was pounding, her breaths rushing in and out of her lungs. If they could catch Samri, Aran, and Vince in the act, with drugged-up girls, then she'd be able to slam a pile of charges on them.

The van came into view, parked between a green motorbike and a skip. The headlights weren't on. The cab was in darkness.

"Be ready for anything," Shona said as they hurried up to it.

"Yeah, these guys are not going to be happy at being caught."

But when they approached, Shona got a sense of unease. There was no life in it, or around it. "Andy, did you see them come to the van?" She set her hand on the cool bonnet.

"No, but I see you there now."

"So where are they?" She spun around, looking at the darkened shop windows and the café all closed up for the night. "Shit. Fuck. Bloody hell. We can't lose them."

"I presumed they'd use this thing." Earle scrubbed his hand over his hair and poked his toe at the van's front tyre. "But if they didn't..."

"Did ANPR pick up the other vehicle? Aran's?"

"No, ma'am. Not to say it wasn't used, though. Ironash isn't thick with surveillance technology."

"Tell me about it." She tutted. In London, she'd been spoilt. "We have to presume they had that parked nearby and that's their getaway vehicle." She pointed up the road. "Back to your car, Earle."

He nodded.

While they ran, Shona barked instructions at Andy. "We're going to Samri's house, to see if that's where the girls have been taken. I want you to send uniforms to Aran's address. Tell them to get there quick, no hanging around. And if they find the bastards, I want as much evidence preserved as possible. SOCO need to be there ASAP."

"Yes, ma'am, on it."

The pressure was on and squeezed Shona's insides as she raced up the hill. When she leapt into Earle's car, she was shaking. Those poor girls were at the mercy of monsters. She had to stop them. She had to catch them. Not doing so wasn't an option.

Earle revved the engine then wheel-span away from the kerb. He hurtled around the corner, flicking on his police lights so the road ahead lit up blue.

Three cars got out of his way, and he skipped through a red, glancing each way to make sure it was safe.

Shona gripped her seat belt and scanned the pavements, checking pedestrians. But there were few people about; it was eleven p.m. after all.

They came to Samri's road. Earle killed the police lights but not the speed until he screeched to a stop.

They both hurtled out, slamming the doors, and legged it up Samri's front path. Like the van, his house was in darkness.

Shona bashed her fist on the door, the sound echoing around the quiet street. "Open up, police," she shouted. She banged again then gave it a shove just in case it was off the latch. It wasn't. "Damn it."

Earle stepped back and stared up at the black windows. "If they're here, there's no lights on."

"Shit." She scraped her fingers into her hair, dragging her nails on her scalp. "We should have gone to Aran's."

"Excuse me?"

She turned at the sound of a quiet voice.

A man, stooped and with a few wisps of hair brushed over the top of an otherwise bald head, leaned against the low fence between Samri's and the house next door.

"Yes?" she asked.

"Are you looking for the resident of this house?"

"Samri Laghari, yes. Do you know where he is?"

"Oh no, I don't know that." He paused, his eyes narrowed. "Who's asking?"

"Police." Earle flashed his ID.

The man's eyes widened. "Ah, okay, well, I have a key to his door if you'd like to use it."

Shona glanced at Earle. He shrugged. "That would be very helpful, thank you."

"He gave me it so I can take in parcels for him. Does a lot of Amazon shopping, you know how young folk are." He held out a Yale key. "He's a decent sort, can't imagine he's got anything to hide from you good people, and if he has...well...he deserves to get caught."

Shona took the key and shoved thoughts of a warrant from her mind. She'd take getting her arse whipped if needed because checking the girls weren't within these walls was her priority.

Quickly, she opened the door. For a moment, before she stepped over the threshold, she paused to steel herself. Samri, Aran, and Vince worked as a well-oiled drugging and raping machine—they wouldn't come easily.

"Want me to go first?" Earle said.

"No, I've got this. Stick close, though."

"Got you."

The first door she came to was open and led to a dark living room with a low sofa, a wall-hung TV, and a coffee table littered with mugs and magazines.

She then had the choice of checking out the kitchen, which was in darkness, or heading up the stairs. She chose the stairs.

The first step creaked, and she paused, listening carefully.

Nothing.

The house appeared to be empty. The silence was wrapping around her like a thick blanket.

"Damn it," she muttered, speeding up with each step until she reached the landing. A bathroom greeted her. Toilet with the lid up, towels on the floor, vague scent of damp.

Earle tapped her shoulder then pointed at a closed door. If she'd worked it out right, that was the biggest bedroom, the one that looked over the street, and where she'd seen what she'd thought was Samri's figure in the window.

She nodded. Stepped up to it. No noises came through the door. Not even a murmur.

As she pushed down the handle, she already knew it would be empty. They'd come to a dead end at this address.

Sure enough, a double bed, unmade, and a wardrobe with one door broken and hanging at an angle was all she found. As well as the scent of aftershave, something from years ago, fruity, was it Joop?

"They're not here?" Desperately, she checked the other room, a small box shape bursting with junk. "Shit, they must be at Aran's." She pulled out her phone and followed Earle down the stairs, her free hand sliding down the wall. "Andy, tell me you've got uniform at Aran Barker's."

"Just arrived."

"And..."

"Give me one minute."

She ended the call and stood in the garden, hands on hips, staring at a flowerbed crammed full of marigolds, their small orange heads seeming to stare up at her.

"Thank you, sir." Earle handed the key back to the waiting neighbour.

"Get what you were searching for?"

"We appreciate your help." Earle shut Samri's front door, clicking it locked. "Nothing else to see here, sir."

"Ah, okay, I'm dismissed. Well, goodnight, keep up the good work, Officer."

Shona paced. Her skin tingled, and her ears rang. Every passing second seemed to increase her blood pressure.

Her phone trilled to life. She answered it instantly. "What?"

"Empty, Aran Barker's place is in darkness, no answer at the door."

"Can they get in?"

"No, but they've been around the back, peered inside. And a neighbour said Aran usually makes it known when he's home—loud music, lots of visitors and the like."

"He wouldn't advertise these visitors."

"What would you like me to do, ma'am?"

"Keep the uniform there and…" Her attention fell on the marigolds again. What was it about them? A thread of a memory slid over her brain. She closed her eyes, tried to pull at it, eke it out from the foggy depths of her mind. But it had been knotted in there tight. Stitched by an expert.

But those tiny, vibrant petals…she'd seen them somewhere. Yes. A marigold had featured in the journey into the basement of her memories when she'd been under hypnosis.

Where had it been?

What was the significance?

Chapter Fifteen

"Buddha?" she said.

"What?" Andy and Earle spoke at the same time.

"Buddha...the curry smell..." She pointed at the flowers. "And marigolds, they're all there. We need to get to it, Earle."

"Get where?" He held out his big palms.

"The restaurant, The Bay Leaf?"

"We do?" He frowned.

"Yes, I'll explain on the way. Andy, send more uniform to The Bay Leaf, now."

"Yes, ma'am."

She was already rushing back to Earle's car.

They both leapt in.

"Are you going to explain?" Earle asked as he did a fast three-point turn, not seeming to care when he mounted the pavement.

"I told you about the hypnosis, right?"

"Yeah." He screeched around a corner, heading back towards the town.

"I thought the smell I remembered was aftershave, *his* aftershave to start with, but then when I went to The Bay Leaf I realised it was the smell of cooking, Indian cooking, spices and curry, you know." She paused, dragged in a breath. "And I saw a Buddha and the mandala under hypnosis."

"Buddha statues, which we've established are everywhere."

"Yes, but the one I saw had marigold heads set around it, like offerings or something."

"So an ornament was being used by someone of faith as opposed to window dressing."

"Exactly, and I saw one exactly like that recently, at—"

"The Bay Leaf." He banged his hand on the steering well. "And combined with the smell, you think that's where you were taken?"

"I'd discounted it, so many restaurants, and why...?" She gripped the door when he took a left turn at maximum speed. "I mean, why there when they have homes?"

"Who knows how their sick minds work, but I'm guessing it's pretty easy to get to on foot from REVS, no need for vehicles at all."

She huffed. "I suppose."

The town was in view. Earle bypassed High Street and pulled into the smaller road The Bay Leaf was on. He parked up.

But even as she got out, Shona's heart was sinking.

The restaurant was in darkness, no lingering customers, or staff, no cars parked up outside.

"I can't believe it." This was hopeless. She'd been so sure. She'd really believed more pieces of the jigsaw from that night had slotted into place.

But they were running out of time to finish the puzzle. If they didn't find the girls soon, their fate would be sealed and their lives would never be the same again.

Earle jogged up to the front entrance of The Bay Leaf. A small sign was taped on the inside of the glass.

"What's it say?" Shona asked, coming to stand at his side.

"Closed for annual holiday. Reopens on tenth of July. To make a booking, call 0789752744."

"Closed for annual holiday," Shona stepped to the kerb and stared up at the mid-terrace building. "Do you think they go away this week every year?"

"Who knows." He took a step behind her and pointed upwards. "Is that a light on, in the roof?"

"A skylight." A rush of hope shot through her as she spotted it. "I think it is." She glanced left and right.

Earle tried the door. "How do we get round the back?"

"I'm guessing there's an alley; these houses just have yards."

"You're right. Come on."

Quickly, they ran past several houses, then turned left. An alley—wide enough for one car—ran down the back of the string of houses.

Shona called Andy. "We're around the back of the restaurant. Send uniform to join us here when they arrive." She was breathless.

"Yes, ma'am. They're a few minutes away."

"We're going in."

Shona and Earle came to a halt at a gate set in a high-bricked wall. She rattled the latch. "Shit, it's locked."

Earle reached over it. He bit on his bottom lip, appeared to feel around, then slid metal on metal. "Now try it."

It opened. "What did you do?"

"It had a bolt. Another advantage of not being a short-arse."

"Hey!"

She whizzed into the small courtyard. It was lined with tall bins. A pile of yellow crates were stacked in the corner. "Yes, look, the same room, don't you think?" She pointed up at another skylight. It was also glowing golden, as though a lamp was on near it.

"Yeah. I'd put money on someone being up there."

"And if the owners are on holiday, it could be our guys."

"But how? Why?"

"Isn't Samri a delivery driver, to restaurants?" She came to a halt at the back door and nodded at the boxes. "I'm guessing he delivers here, knows the annual holiday routine and…" she tried to door, it was locked, "and he has a key."

A siren sounded in the distance.

"Backup's on the way."

"I'm not waiting." How could she? Those girls had been at the mercy of monsters for too long as it was. "Are you going to break this door down or am I, DS?"

"In for a penny, in for a pound. We're already likely to get in shit for searching without a warrant."

"I don't mind taking the rap."

"One property each." He eased her to one side, bunched his shoulder against the wooden frame, then rammed his weight into it.

The door popped open.

They both stilled, held their breath. Had they given themselves away?

But after a few seconds, with no movement from the building and the siren getting louder, they stepped in, Shona in the lead.

Once more, the sickly sweet scent of cardamom, cumin, chilli, and coconut hit her. She stepped farther inside.

She'd been in this corridor recently when out with her new karate friends, but she'd entered from the opposite end, the restaurant end. To her right was a kitchen, and she paused to peer inside. It was all industrial steel and polished white tiles. A huge hob and a large island towered in the centre. It appeared spotlessly clean.

"Where's the stairs?" Earle whispered.

"Just along here, near the toilets." She led the way and paused when she spotted the doglegged stairway. The Buddha was still there, halfway up, with a window behind him. No marigolds this time, not like when she'd been dragged up here, drugged and out of it. But there was an incense stick, burnt out, and on a holder with an engraved lotus flower. "Come on, we need to hurry."

"We'll have company soon. The siren might spook them."

"I agree, but my guess is they're cocky bastards, they think they're safe up there." She climbed the stairs, went past the first floor and up the next level into what she guessed was an area that used to be an attic.

A single door led from a tiny landing at the top of the stairs. A slash of light pierced the base, spilling onto the worn carpet.

Voices.

Deep male voices.

Shona looked at Earle who stood on the top step, one hand on the wall.

Through the darkness, his features were tense, his eyes flashing. His adrenaline was tearing though his veins the same way hers was.

"We're going in," she said, "Right?"

Fletcher would tell us to wait for backup.

"Right." He nodded. "We can't…"

He didn't need to finish the sentence. They couldn't wait, not another second.

Shona gripped the handle, hoped uniform had their best running shoes on, and opened the door.

The first thing her attention settled on was a great big wall hanging directly in front of her. Red, yellow, blue, and orange, it was a mandala, *the* mandala. Her muscles seemed to turn to stone, fear gripped her heart, and in her mind she saw the face of the man who'd drugged and abused her.

And then she saw him for real, lunging at her.

"What the fuck. You!" he shouted.

She rushed to meet him. In her peripheral vision, she spotted more figures standing, some on a bed.

His fist flew at her face. She blocked it and got a jab in on the end of his nose. He reeled backwards, blood spurting as he staggered and yelped.

"Who the hell are you?" Another man. Aran Barker.

"Police, you're all under arrest." Earle stepped past her but stayed blocking the door.

"We haven't done nothing wrong." Aran put his hands on his hips and tilted his chin. There was a ripe spot on the end. "We're just having fun with our girlfriends. No law against sex, even if it is kinky as fuck."

"The law has a major bloody problem when they're out of it." Shona pointed to the bed.

Two naked girls sat nestled together. Their wrists were tied with rough brown rope. One was asleep, her head on the shoulder of the other. The awake one, whose long blonde hair stuck messily to her cheek, appeared to be struggling to keep her eyes open. Her focus had gone, and a length of drool ran from her mouth.

"Bitch!" Samri suddenly lunged at Shona again. There was madness in his eyes, and he had his hands curled, as though about to strangle her.

Shona dodged to the right and packed a kidney punch in. She probably shouldn't have, but it felt good.

He yelped and turned, his body listing as he gripped his right side and shoulder-bumped the wall.

"What, you don't recognise me now I can fight?" she asked.

"As the police bitch who took me down at the festival when I'd done nothing wrong. The whore who tried to ruin my reputation. Yeah, course I do."

"Ah, so not as a girl you drugged and raped eight years ago?" She placed her hands on her hips.

"What?" He stilled. His eyes widened, and his mouth fell open.

"Shit, man." Vince spoke for the first time.

He stood beside another single bed. On it was a girl, her hands tied to a headboard so her torso was stretched. She still wore knickers, though her head lolled, lips parted as if she was unconscious, and her breasts rose and fell with her shallow breaths.

We need medical help. Fast.

"You took a policewoman, you fucking knob!" Vince rushed forward. For a moment, it looked like he was going for Samri, but then he veered to the door.

But Earle was there. He swept Vince's feet from under him and knocked him to the floor.

Vince went down hard, the air grunting up from his lungs. But despite this, he tried to sit.

Earle pressed his huge boot on his chest and glared down at him. "Do you really think you can get away from me, arsehole?"

Vince stared up at him, teeth gritted, and shook his head.

"And I've got two boots," Earle directed at Aran. "So if you want some of this, try it."

Earle applied pressure.

Vince gripped Earle's ankle and groaned.

"You're off your trolley. You can't just barge in here and attack us." Samri shook his fist at Earle then turned to Shona. "I'll sue your arses for this. I know my rights."

"Every year, this week, for the last eight, you've drugged three women." Shona held her hand out to Earle.

He tossed her a set of handcuffs.

She caught them with a snap of her hand. "Three women, all of whom were just out for a nice time. A dance, a drink, a gossip with friends. Yet what you and your sick mates have done." She paused at the sound of footsteps on the floors below. "What you've done, in this room, each year, has wrecked lives, broken minds, and shattered dreams." She opened the cuffs. "But me…you made a mistake there. I refused to be broken, refused to give up, until, that is, I'd broken you and your cronies." She nodded at his hands. "Hold them up."

He didn't.

She raised her eyebrows. "And you will be broken. In jail. You'll go down for not just years, but decades."

"There's no evidence."

"You're not as clever as you think. I have plenty of evidence."

He appeared to pale a little, his coffee-skin lightening a fraction. "You're bluffing."

"I guess you'll find out."

The footsteps were getting louder.

Samri glanced at the door.

"I'm going to have you taken down to the station," Shona said, "and charged with multiple accounts of date rape, kidnap, and one murder."

"Murder. I didn't fucking murder anyone."

She thought of Nicola, how she'd been unable to face the world after her night in this hateful room with these hateful men. "I'm not sure a jury will see it that way."

"That's shit. I didn't." He backed up, hitting the wall. There was fear in his eyes now.

Good. He deserves fear, terror, panic, the lot. He deserves to rot in Hell for all eternity. So do his friends.

Two uniformed officers appeared at the door, breathing hard. A male and female.

"I'm DI Williams, new around here," Shona said.

"What do you want us to do, ma'am?"

"Can you get cuffs on that one." She pointed at Aran who stood like a deer in headlights in the corner. He was shirtless, and a tattoo curved from one skinny collarbone to the other. 'Son of Death'.

The male officer stepped up to him, whipping cuffs from his belt. He was tall and thickset. Aran didn't give him any trouble.

"The women." Shona nodded at the girls.

But the female PC was already moving, grasping a blanket as she rushed to them. She put it around their shoulders, tugging it tight, then swiftly went to the bed and covered the girl there. "Ambulance, ma'am?"

"Yes." Shona nodded.

"They asked for this," Samri said. "They're our girlfriends, they like a bit of rough on a Saturday night."

"We'll ask them when the rohypnol is out of their system." Shona put her hands on her hips.

"What rohypnol?" He swallowed. "I don't even know what that shit is."

"Luckily our forensic doctors do." She stepped closer, cuffs once more at the ready.

He made a weird roaring sound, energy bursting from him, and he seemed to rise upwards, fly, in a manic bid to reach the door.

Shona didn't hesitate. She chased him, the way she had at the festival. In three fast strides, she was next to him and kicked his feet from under him. He fell back, towards her, so she allowed his torso to roll down the length of her thighs, spinning him faster so his impact with the floor gusted the air from him and his head bounced off the carpet.

He stared up at her, shock searing over his eyes as he dragged in a pathetically wheezy breath.

She pulled back her fist. His nose was already bloody, but damn, she wanted to mess it up big time. Knock a few teeth out, too, create a couple more gaps. His evil buggy eyes could do with...

"Shona."

Earle's voice cut through her pulse raging in her ears.

"Shona," he said again.

She dropped to her knees, grabbed Samri's wrists, and snapped the cuffs on. After a few deep breaths, she read him his rights—a moment she'd waited a long time for. "Samri Laghari, you're under arrest for..."

Chapter Sixteen

Shona paced Fletcher's office. Her arms were crossed tight, and her stomach gurgled. She was tense, het up—the three cups of coffee hadn't helped.

Earle and Fletcher were downstairs in the interrogation rooms. They'd been at it all morning with Aran Barker, Vince Thomas, and Samri Laghari. There was a lot to go through, a lot to charge them with.

As a victim of one of their crimes, Shona wasn't legally allowed to be involved in the questioning process. Her job was done. All she could do now was sit back—or pace—and pray they all got maximum sentencing when the time came.

Her phone rang. "Hi, Dad?"

"Hey, sweetheart, we didn't hear you come in last night, and then the only evidence that you'd been home was a muesli bar wrapper on the kitchen table this morning."

"Yes, sorry. It was a late one."

He was silent.

She swallowed, steadied her voice. "I got them, Dad. All of them." For the first time since the arrest, her eyes pricked with tears. She squeezed the bridge of her nose and pressed her lips in on themselves.

He breathed deep, a shaky inhalation down the line. "Good for you. Good for you." He paused. "I never doubted that you would, though."

"Thanks, you and Mum have been great." She paused to ensure she still had control of her voice. "All this time, I knew I had your support, it helped me keep going."

"In whatever you decide to do. You'll always have our support."

She released the pinch on her nose and stared out of the window at the police car park. "I know. And I know I've put you through a lot—"

"Stop it. You need to celebrate. Give yourself a pat on the back. We're hugely proud of you and how you've shown unwavering focus to put those scumbags away. That night shaped your life, yes, but you didn't let it beat you." He paused. "We'll always be grateful that our daughter was the strong one."

She sniffed. It was there, the sob.

"And tonight, we'll go out and celebrate," he went on. "A nice meal somewhere. An Indian, fancy that? The Bay Leaf is supposed to be good."

She laughed, a fast expulsion of air which released tension. "The meal sounds lovely, but not there, Dad, and not tonight. I have somewhere to be."

"Tomorrow?"

"That would be great."

"We're on. I'll book Amico Chef, they do a great lasagne, and your mum loves the prawn salad."

"I'm already looking forward to it. Say hi to Mum. See you later." She hung up.

The office door opened. Fletcher and Earle walked in. Both seemed tired. Fletcher's tie was askew, something she hadn't seen before.

"Well?" she asked, slipping her phone away and recrossing her arms. She gripped her biceps through her blue cotton blouse.

"We're not finished," Earle said. "Not by a long shot."

"But what have you got so far?"

Fletcher set a stack of files on his desk. "I'll leave Earle to fill you in," he said with a quick nod. "I have to speak to Darren about a couple of things and then get to the hospital."

"Of course, sir." When Fletcher had shut the office door, Earle took a seat and set his hand over the files. With his fingers spread, it practically covered them.

"He okay?" She nodded at the closed door.

"He's a professional bloke, been in the job for years, but those men, what they did and how they are, their attitude." He pursed his lips and blew out a breath. "And knowing they did it to one of our own... Let's just say it's pushing even the most experienced copper I know."

She shuddered as a wave of discomfort tickled its way up her spine. She'd never shake the shame of the assault. It was something she had to live with. And knowing that two of her colleagues now knew all the details was uncomfortable to the point she squirmed.

But it was a necessity.

"Any of them cracked with the other cases?" She pulled in a deep breath.

Earle lifted the top file up. "Aran Barker, he's the squealer of the threesome. I told him he'd get a lighter sentence if he talked and I guess he knew he'd been caught red-handed so had nothing to lose."

She waited for him to go on.

"He confessed to all the abductions though claims he was never the one to administer the rohypnol."

"That was Samri every time, I bet."

Earle nodded. "He also confessed to multiple indecent assaults and five counts of rape. Implicated the other two men on every occasion as his accomplices."

"Good." She forced herself to uncross her arms. She was going to give herself bruises, or pull a muscle.

"Did find out something interesting, though, and I've had a PC go to REVS and check."

"Oh?"

"He used his electrician status to fool them into thinking he was servicing the CCTV. All he did was set it on a timer, a simple one, on the plug. It was set to turn the camera system off at eleven o'clock for one hour—that was their time to get away without being caught on film."

"But they miss-timed it last night by what...fifteen seconds."

"Yep, they did. Thank goodness." He tapped the folder. "Like I said, I can't shut him up now."

"There's more."

"Yeah, The Bay Leaf shuts for this week in the summer every year. The owners go to visit family abroad."

"And Samri is one of their suppliers—"

"And, as you suspected, he has a key for dropping off deliveries. Aran said they knew they'd be undisturbed there, and with the secluded back alley into the place, and a short walk or stagger from town, they made the most of it, every time."

"Bastards," she muttered, thinking of all the years they'd got away with it.

"The girls from last night are doing fine, by the way. Fletcher's going to take statements, that's why he's gone to the hospital."

"He is?" Not usual DCI work.

"He wants to make sure we nail these scumbags on every charge we can."

"I'm not going to complain about that, but...really, we just made it in time. Imagine if we hadn't figured it out and—"

"But you did, and we were, so there's no point thinking that." His voice was low and deep. "Now onto Vince Thomas. He's already got a suspended for GBH as we know. He's really not a nice bloke to be in the same room as, and as he's proven, not one you want to meet in a dark alley either."

Again, she turned to the window. This time she looked at the little Buddha on the sill.

"Vince isn't as chatty as his mate, Aran, even with the DNA evidence thrust in his face, but I can see it in his eyes that he knows he has no defence, he's guilty as sin. It's only a matter of time till he cracks or a solicitor cracks him."

She turned back to the room then leaned against the sill, gripping it. "And Samri?"

Her attacker.

"I got a warrant first thing, sent SOCO round to go through his place with a fine-tooth comb."

"Anything yet?"

"Oh yeah. A stash of date-rape drugs of suspect quality, weed, several burner phones, some particularly nasty porn, and..."

"And what?"

"A bag stuffed full of female clothes." He rubbed his bottom lip. "Fancy ones, going out, clubbing clothes. Sparkly little dresses, high heels and the like."

"Shit, really?" Could her outfit from that night be there? Tina's and Nicola's, too? "So they were his souvenirs? We were all dumped naked and he kept our clothes."

"That's what I'm thinking."

"Wow." She pushed from the windowsill and paced to the desk. She set her palms on it and shook her head as she stared down at a blank notepad. "Stupid bastard."

"But good news for us."

"When can I see the clothing?"

"To identify yours? Tomorrow."

"Okay, I can live with that." She knew full well they'd be there—Tina's sparkly top, Nicola's little black dress, her own red mini skirt.

"So you can see." Earle stood. "We're making excellent progress. They won't be seeing the light of day for a very long time. Their list of crimes is eye-watering. You can be confident that these arseholes are going down, right here, right now."

She closed her eyes, then straightened and knotted her fingers beneath her chin. "I've dreamed of this."

"I know, and I'm sorry you did it alone for so long."

"You have nothing to be sorry about. If it hadn't been for you, Earle." She opened her eyes and focused on him. "I'm not sure last night would have been the success it was."

"Nonsense, I was just the brawn." He grinned and held out his arms.

"What?" She frowned at him.

"You look like you need a hug."

"You know I'm not a huggy person." Her frown deepened. Her heart was thudding, and her knees and spine felt weak, as if the joints had been replaced with dust.

Has this really finally happened?

Earle waggled his brows comically. "Ah, but this isn't just a hug…this is an Earle Montague hug."

Shona burst out laughing, then stepped up to him.

He wrapped her in his arms. She didn't hug him back, kept her hands tucked beneath her chin, but she allowed herself to lean against his warm, wide chest.

"You've shown amazing strength," he said quietly, "and incredible dedication to getting justice for yourself, your friends, and the other victims. Maybe now it's time to exhale."

She didn't reply. She wasn't ready to exhale just yet.

There was still something else to do. And it was incredibly important.

* * * *

Shona drove the forty-five minutes to Haversham Psychiatric Unit in silence. No music, no radio, just lost in her thoughts.

When she arrived at the old stately home, she parked by a huge expanse of emerald lawn. She got out, walked over the gravel, then said hello to a nurse and a patient in a wheelchair heading down a paved path.

She had to press an intercom to get into reception, and once there was greeted with another locked door and a receptionist behind a glass screen.

It had been over six months since she'd visited and didn't recognise the male member of staff.

"Hi, I'm here to see Tina Berry, please."

"It's not visiting day, that's tomorrow."

"I thought it was every day, every afternoon."

"Nope, rules changed."

"Oh." Damn it. "I've driven from Ironash."

"Come back tomorrow." He didn't glance up from his phone.

Just rude.

Shona's hackles rose—she was tired, no, make that she was exhausted, and all out of patience. "What's your name?"

He glanced up. His glasses were perched on the end of his nose, and he had a strawberry-shaped birthmark on his jawline. "What?"

"What's your name?" She didn't bother to try to inject politeness into her tone.

He pointed at a slime white badge pinned to his blue shirt.

"Derek." She forced a smile. "I'm actually not *asking* you if I can visit Tina Berry, I'm *telling* you." She produced her ID and held it at the window. "DI Shona Williams, I'm here on police business."

"Oh." He sat up straighter. "I'm sorry, you should have said."

"I just have." She bit on her bottom lip to prevent herself from giving him a lecture on attitude. She just didn't have the energy today.

"In that case, go ahead, Inspector. Would you like someone to accompany you?"

"No, thank you. She's in room forty-one, I believe, first floor."

"Yes, doesn't come out of it."

"By choice?"

"By choice." He nodded.

"Damn," she muttered. No progress since her last visit then. But perhaps she could change that with her news.

The door buzzed to release the lock, and Shona stepped into the grand foyer. A polished wooden banister lined a wide staircase, and several plush plants sat in huge ceramic pots. A red patterned rug was positioned squarely in the centre of the floor. To the right, a door set in the wood-panelled walls was open a fraction. *Nurses Office* was written on a brass plaque.

Shona took to the stairs, withdrawing her phone. She flicked it to silent. The last thing she wanted was to be interrupted on this visit—she'd been planning it for years.

She reached the top and turned right. At the end of the corridor, a huge window was lit by the sun, and it flickered as the branches of a tree swayed before it, casting jumping shadows on the floor and walls.

She reached room forty-one. The door was closed. Taking a deep breath, she knocked softly.

No answer.

She knocked again. "Tina?"

"Who is it?" A quiet, shaky voice.

"It's me, Shona."

The door opened.

Tina stood there, thin, pale, and her black t-shirt—with the image of a small bee and the words Bee Kind—hung off her shoulders. She smiled, not a big smile, and it didn't reach her eyes, but at least she'd got up off the bed and opened the door. More than last time. Perhaps there was some hope, still some light, even if it was weak.

"I'm sorry it's been so long since my last visit," Shona said.

"Has it?"

"Yes, six months. I've been busy."

Tina didn't say anything. Instead, she turned and sat on her narrow bed which was pushed up against the wall. Her shoulders hunched, and she clasped her hands on her lap.

Shona shut the door. The room had a huge, lead-paned window which showcased the summer sky and the stately gardens dotted with ancient oaks. "These paintings are great." The room was stacked with them. All of the same image—the window and the gardens. But instead of blue skies with fluffy marshmallow clouds, they were more Turner-esq with bruised storms slashing over the canvas, fierce winds curving the branches of bare trees.

Shona was sure the Haversham psychologists had a field day with the symbolism.

"I've been told to paint what I see." She nodded to the window.

"Have you ever thought about painting the sky blue?" Shona sat on the bed beside her.

"Blue?"

"Yes, like it is today."

Tina glanced to her right. She seemed surprised to see the azure sky, then, "I'm not painting today."

"So what are you doing?"

"Nothing, my arm is sore." She rubbed the left one.

Shona had no idea if that was the truth or just what she said when she didn't want to paint. She'd always been good at art. Once upon a time her plan had been to go to art and design college.

A silence stretched between them. Shona wondered if Tina might fill it.

She didn't.

"Tina," she said, having to stop herself reaching for Tina's hand. Her friend didn't like to be touched these days. Shona could relate to that. "I have something to tell you."

Still silence.

"We've caught them." She let the words sink in, or at least she hoped they were. "We caught all three of the men who took us that night."

Very slowly, Tina turned to face her.

"It took me a while." Shona chose her words carefully. "But I promised you I would catch them, put them in jail, and I have."

Tina blinked, twice. "You caught them?"

How much is she registering?

"Yes, you remember, I'm a policewoman now."

"Yes. Yes." She nodded—it was the fastest movement Shona had seen in a long time. "I remember."

"We, me and my partner, we followed them, caught them, gathered evidence, and now they'll be going to court. A judge will put them behind bars for years and years." She itched to stroke Tina's lank hair. "They can't hurt you anymore, they can't hurt anyone, Tina."

She turned to the window.

Shona studied her profile. She'd always adored Tina's little pixie nose and delicate features.

"They're…they're not out there?" she asked.

"No, they're in Ironash Police Station, in the cells. From there, they'll be taken away until the trial."

"They're not out there," she repeated.

"No. Which means *you* can go out again." She held her breath. How would Tina react to that suggestion?

She stood and walked to the window, pulled up her jeans, which were slipping down her skinny hips.

Shona breathed out and also stood. A sense of calmness was coming over her. She'd done all of this for Tina, and Nicola, too, but mainly so Tina could get on with her life. Overcome her terror of the outside world, of strangers, of crowds, open spaces, drink of any sort, the dark; the list went on.

"Maybe today," Tina said eventually. "I will paint after all."

"And what colour will the sky be?" Shona held her breath.

"The sky is blue, the sun is bright." She inhaled, set her shoulders back, and tilted her chin upwards. "Yes, I can see it now. Perfect blue, and the sun so, so bright."

Shona exhaled.

Thank you, God.

She sat with Tina for another forty minutes as she started to paint. There wasn't much conversation, but there was still more than the last time she'd been to Haversham.

When she said goodbye, she promised to visit again the next week—it would be much easier now she wasn't living and working in London.

Walking back to her car she felt lighter—it was easier to stand tall; walking was no longer like going into battle.

She got in her car and moved the bunch of pink and white flowers out of the direct sunlight. They were for her next port of call, the cemetery.

She turned on her phone. It flashed with two new messages. The first was from Bethany.

It was so good to bump into you at REVS. Lunch on Saturday? Bethany xx

Shona reread it. It was such a simple message. Nothing more than a friend wanting to spend time with her.

Her usual instinct was to say no. Too busy. Too much work on. Sleep was a priority. But not this time. Bethany was nice, good fun, there was no reason not to hang out.

Saturday is perfect. Text me your address. I'll pick you up at one. Shona xx

She hit 'send' before she could change her mind. Lunch with a friend was a normal thing to do, and now was the perfect moment to start being more normal.

She opened her next message.

It was from Ben.

Shona, sorry about Friday at Grapes Ahoy, I have no right to an opinion on where you are or who you are with. I hope you'll still come to the dojo for tonight's training session. I'd really love to see you and apologise in person. Ben.

She stared out of the window. Two rabbits were grazing in the shade of a tree.

She'd seen hurt in Ben's eyes that night at the wine bar, not anger. He'd asked her out then seen her with another bloke when she'd said she was busy with work. What man wouldn't be confused?

She drafted a reply.

It's not what you think. I was with my partner, we were working. A big case, and I needed to concentrate. I'm sorry for not explaining, though you didn't give me much chance. Shona.

She went over it again.

Hit 'delete'.

Apology not necessary, and yes, I'll be at training tonight. Looking forward to it. Shona xx

She sent, realising afterwards that she'd added the two kisses at the end, the way she had replied to Bethany's text.

She smiled and started the engine. Oh well. Ben was cute, his smile was infectious, and he smelt nice. Perhaps one of these days—if she got time between hunting out serial killers and madmen—she would kiss him for real.

THE END

ABOUT IRONASH

Ironash is a fictional town in the heart of England, now kept safer by the return of DI Shona Williams. And it's just as well, a lot of bad shit happens there!

#1 Sin, Repent, Repeat

#2 The Last Post

#3 Blind Panic

Follow A. J. Harlem on Amazon to get an alert when new books are released in the IRONASH series.

About the Author

A. J. Harlem is a bestselling author who has opened her vivid imagination to create thrilling British detective novels. She's always lived in the UK —England, Scotland, and currently South Wales—and adores the colloquial use of the English language and quintessential settings for murder, crime, and high drama. When she isn't writing, her favourite pastimes generally revolve around her love of animals and include horse riding on the beach, walking her dogs in the Welsh mountains, and flying birds of prey.